JOY

'My name is Joy, I am twenty-two, tall, slender, and a natural blonde. Being blonde I attract men – but why do I never get the nice ones? Once I submitted eagerly to the homage paid to my beauty – but then I was just a fool strutting about on the edge of an abyss ...'

JOY

A novel by Joy Laurey
Translated by Celeste Piano

A STAR BOOK
Published by
the Paperback Division of
W. H. Allen & Co. Ltd

A Star Book
Published in 1983
by the Paperback Division of
W. H. Allen & Co. Ltd
A Howard and Wyndham Company
44 Hill Street, London W1X 8LB

First published in France by Éditions Robert Laffont, 1981

Copyright © Éditions Robert Laffont, S. A., Paris 1981
Translation copyright © Star Books 1983

Printed in Great Britain by
Hunt Barnard Printing Ltd., Aylesbury, Bucks.

ISBN 0 352 31454 0

Love is full of contradictions . . .

CHAPTER ONE

I have never understood men at all. I've confused things as in
a badly learned lesson, without reflecting or paying attention,
and so I've blundered along making mistakes and ruining
everything. I used to be the life and soul of the party,
Superwoman, sweety-pie, everyone's favourite, the pre-
destined winner, quite the little treasure ... I was absolutely
oblivious of the pain that brutal, bruising love can cause. As
for middle-aged passion, late loves whether sad or perverse –
all that sort of thing provoked my derision and I gave it short
shrift. Attractive as I was, I couldn't have been more stupid.
Yet I *was* happy, happy and empty.

Now I live in the past, scared of saying goodbye to the
soothing green pastures of adolescence. I can still taste the
tang of those days and savour the bitter-sweet quality of those
youthful floods of tears. If I close my eyes I can rediscover my
mother's softness: my nose is buried in her pullover, while the
pink glow from the lamp-shade lends my room the colour of
an acid drop. That was the era of vanilla, chocolate and
blackcurrant syrup, of teeth proudly and individually lost.
There were sugar mice, caramels, the enticing aromas of jams
in glass jars with handwritten labels. Hours passed
wonderfully slowly then, ambushed only by a large brass
pendulum shining through the half-light of those drowsy
summer afternoons, when shutters were closed to trap the
coolness indoors and I would usually be found lounging on

7

the comfortable flowered sofa.

It took me a century or so to reach the age of twenty. A mass of faded sensations pressed like dried flowers between the pages of a secret diary. ... Memories seem to pursue me, catching me up as soon as I am on my own. One word, a snatch of music – and it seems I'm looking over my shoulder again. Occasionally the mention of some half-familiar yet strange or foreign name mysteriously disturbs or threatens me and for a while an unbearable unease upsets the languid game of patience my life has become. I conquer my depressions with the desperation of a sailor forced to fight a storm, but find that I return obsessively to my childhood home in which each object, with a life of its own, is waiting for me. My dolls still wear their stiff taffeta frocks, rats still scurry through the attic, the small front-door bell tinkles whenever the wind blows, birds dip into the guttering with their beaks and the cockerel still crows himself hoarse. Nothing will ever stop in my absence, although I was forgotten the moment I departed, a passenger in transit. ... When your connection is announced, no time remains in which to unpack your luggage.

I am twenty-two, yet I've lived too fast, I've been on the wrong track. A fatal error. I should have become a bourgeois housewife by now, dedicated to bringing up children as straight as the father who'd boss them about. I would have dazzled at endless dinners, drawing sidelong glances from admirers. I'd have known the pleasure of doing the housework on the maid's day off. On those days only, I might lovingly have reheated the spring vegetable soup supposed to put colour in the cheeks of all nicely brought up children. To the neighbour's greetings, I'd have replied with that slightly suggestive jauntiness which smug, smartly-dressed women exude. I would have lived in a provincial town with leafy promenades, a place whose whole tone was lofty yet insulated and bland, where conventions and good manners were still ruled by and expressed in the pluperfect subjunctive. I might have known the intoxicating adventure of the yearly trip to Paris – where the longsuffering and despised lover would be waiting for me. The man who knew just how to humiliate my hypocritical body with earth-shattering pleasure ... I ought and could have experienced all that.

Instead I was turned into a beauty. I had everything going for me: bright personality, figure, looks, whatever drove men wild, made them brutal and menacing or turned them into lovers, suitors, hunters, shy or sly, embarrassing or embarrassed, cavemen or clowns. How often I prayed for an ugly nose, a nutcracker chin, a low forehead or a rougher skin – so that by divine transformation I would no longer be the sort of beautiful girl whose looks caused sleepless nights. I wanted to be, if not exactly ugly, somehow less attractive: to attain that insignificance which characterizes submissive wives and embittered spinsters. For as long as I can remember I was saddled with meaningless adjectives. From the very start I have been, in turn, a hussy and a scamp, precocious and perverse. Then I was told I had 'that certain look' or that I led men on. I became 'provocative', a vamp, a cockteaser. Recently I rose to the rank of 'exhibitionist'. Indeed, I understood early enough that it took only a single gesture or a look to disturb those adults I was impressed by, and in this way they were vulnerable.

I learned to laugh provocatively, to flutter my eyelashes and sigh soulfully. In the pink solitude of my room, I would practise for hours, trying out meaningful glances and swinging my hips. I worked at turning the head very slowly letting a thoughtful expression linger so that my artfully placed if somewhat worn mirrors would duly multiply it. I rehearsed hard: quivering breathily, placing a hand lightly to my neck, fluttering my fingers, delicately frowning and seductively arching my plucked eyebrows. When I was sure I had found a good pose, I would rush to try it out upon the immaculate and callow youths who paid my mother daily visits in the futile hope of catching me unawares. I analysed my triumphs and savoured my victories.

I loved to witness the discomfort of some earnest sporty type twisting around in the upright chair. I mercilessly compounded my victim's embarrassment by means of a shameless stare straight into his tormented features. I never could abide hearty types. A sportsman-lover only underlines, for me, a contradiction in terms. I became *irresistible* and men simply fell at my feet! Coquette and capricious egoist; a cold, scornful cynical flirt; perverse, lying, fickle: I pulled every trick on them. You think I'm a slut? It's worse than that, for in hindsight I feel both shame and mortification. But between these ballbreaking triumphs and the misery I wallow in today, something happened which I could not keep to myself. I tried, however. I made many excuses to friends and acquaintances, not to mention reporters from the tabloids and mass-market weeklies – to keep silent about the bewildering adventure which transformed a well-known and sought-after model into something of a disaster area. Now I give in. I'll tell all, as they say.

I am not one of those women who claim to know how to write a book or who treat their dirty linen like the Turin Shroud. I don't know how a confession should start. Let's try this: I'm twenty-two and my name is Joy.

My father was an American and mother, tactful soul, settled upon a name more American than French. That particular complication is the only thing my father ever did give me, however indirectly. Soon afterwards he departed and we never saw him again. I never knew him and my mother had not even had time to take a photo of him. A rainy Easter Bank holiday weekend at Croix-de-Vie in the Vendée and he bequeathed me as a souvenir.

Born of an unknown father, I invented a father for myself, a father to suit my juvenile imagination: a real blond cowboy, doughty redresser of wrongs who could build a log cabin with his own bare hands, break in a wild bronco and with just a word calm all my distress and anxiety. For a long time I believed he would show up at the school gate and carry me off in a green Cadillac bristling with aerials, but he never appeared. I am sure he's living somewhere in France. Maybe in Paris, quite near my *quartier*, even at the corner of my street perhaps – sublimely unaware of the little miracle he conceived during a wet Easter at Croix-de-Vie. Often when I pass a tall fairhaired man I half turn, my heart pounding, ready to hail my father, but these tall blond men always move on without looking back. Mother told me he was very handsome, but she always exaggerates a little.

I adore my mother. She gave me all the love in the world and then some, you might say. Our relationship has always been both ambiguous and involved: passions either rose high or were cooled by the interminable and pathetic shared silences that hung between us. Then we'd eat out together (spaghetti at the local Italian place), and later even sleep in the same bed, where she'd cradle and cuddle me and sometimes sing me a song. Mother resembles Romy Schneider when she sings – same eyes, same expression – and is not at all like me. She's a blonde whose hair has a reddish tinge. Her mouth is rather too full and she has just a hint of buck teeth. Mine are almost like that too, set wide apart and very white. I'm always told I have beautiful teeth, but I consider them too big: I'd have preferred smaller teeth, like a child's milk teeth in fact, but mine are too prominent for my liking.

My mother lives with a redhaired Swiss who wears bifocals. I can't abide him. He's humourless and uptight, a gingery creature quite the opposite of the macho blond cowboy image, and he's weighed down with the usual chequebooks and credit cards in true Switzer style. A sad character and one who'd really like to peer up my skirt: the moment he finds himself alone with me he seems almost to drool at the mouth. We've steered clear of each other since the notorious evening when, encouraged by a glass or two of lukewarm champagne, he thrust me back against the settee laughing unpleasantly, while mother was stirring the *fondue* in the kitchen. He pulled up my dress and tried to stroke my thighs – before mother came in unexpectedly to find me leaning forward with my skirt hoisted up to my buttocks while he grovelled over my knees with one shaking hand groping at the white triangle of my knickers. I'll always remember how she looked then, pathetic yet dignified, carrying the steaming *fondue* dish, as she exclaimed with a smile: "Come on, behave yourselves, you're too old for children's games!"

I felt stricken. Albert laughed loudly, his spectacles quite steamed up, while mother's attitude seemed to imply: *They're all the same, Joy, you mustn't take it amiss, you're so pretty, he couldn't resist, the champagne was tepid but never mind, it's not important, we understand each other, you and I. . . .*

Ever since then, I've disliked *fondue*. And I visit mother in her depressing Avenue de Breteuil flat only when Albert is in Lausanne.

At twenty-two, I'm blonde and blue-eyed, like millions of other women. My so-called perverse look is actually due to short sight, for I'm as blind as a bat. When I forget my schoolmarm glasses, I can't see a bus twenty yards away: dreams and reality become confused. It is not easy to describe oneself but that is part of setting the record straight, so if you find it of interest, here goes. I am tall and slender. My breasts are shapely – full and rounded (thanks no doubt to my American blood), for I've drunk gallons of milk in my day, which makes for bigger breasts – did you know, by the way, that American women have large bosoms because they drink too much milk? My breasts are firm and the nipples jut slightly upwards. I'm happy with them and fondle them often for I've got very sensitive tits that respond to the slightest touch.

I am a natural blonde. I don't know why brunettes are so jealous of blondes. Blondes never talk of dyeing their hair raven black, it's true, although most brunettes do fantasize about Scandinavian blondeness. I don't understand that, since I think dark-haired women look great. As luck would have it, my rivals have invariably been brunettes and I've never known any particularly well. Being blonde I attract men but never the nice ones. A natural blonde, it seems, is a curiosity. The first time a man undresses me, he goes into ecstasies of comparison and comment. I remember once when a man fell at my knees, gasping: "You're all pink and golden!" and his eyes positively glazed over.

A beautiful object, like a work of art, is worth going out of one's way to admire. I used to submit eagerly to the homage paid to my beauty, for I was just a fool strutting about on the brink of the abyss.

Then, without warning, I lost my appetite, my smile and my peace of mind. I no longer told funny stories at smart dinner parties. I stopped playing pranks – like slipping ice cubes down my admirers' shirts. I never enjoyed a good cry any more over obscure foreign movies. I seemed to age a thousand years in a day, with wrinkles and bags appearing under my eyes. I was in love.

In fact I was overwhelmed and utterly destroyed – while for four long and unrelenting years I was in love with just one man. He had only to snap his fingers and I'd come running, crawling: I was ready to drop everything, quite unconditionally. He could mould me to his will – I'd accept, sign the contract sight unseen, abandoning my rights, making him a gift of myself, renouncing my freedom. My lover resembled no other: he was handsomer, stronger, finer, or so I thought, which was why I took up with him. I was endlessly and absolutely available. Our love was surreal and weird and thanks to him I'll carve my own little mythical niche, alongside Sade's Juliette, Héloïse – and all the other fruit ripe for plucking.

Marc Charroux wherever you are, I hope the vitriol of these memoirs will strike you down and you will never forget what I *might* have been ... You liar. You mediocrity. You *married man*. Safely married, two point four children: that's your epitaph, you phony.

Mother had warned me. "Keep away from married men. They're liars and selfish brutes and you'll waste your life on them since all they ever do is run away: every time you think you've won, you'll see them leave you. Married men are men without weekends, they slink back home at dead of night, running out while you're asleep. They don't even kiss you for fear of waking you up. When you open your eyes, you're alone

13

with that lingering pleasure which weighs so heavily that it seems almost stifling. Joy my love, married men mean perpetual flight, furtive phone calls, restaurants that must be avoided, trips endlessly postponed, Christmases spent alone, New Year's Eve on the rocks. You may snatch a week here or there if you're lucky – bed and breakfast, always under a false name, in some obscure resort – and never during school holidays.

"Married men are illusionists who always want to be in two different places at once, but their tricks never quite come off and they never succeed in escaping from their trunks bound with chains. That enigmatic look of theirs only reflects their preoccupation with the single tiny detail overlooked, an obsession with the fatal grain of sand clogging up their otherwise perfect arrangements. They say Perhaps rather than Yes, and qualify everything with If. They're gram- marians – of the future conditional – and expert architects when it comes to shoring up the lies. They cultivate insincerity: *But you saw me*, they'll complain, *that's not possible, I wasn't there, not with her, I swear to you, cross my heart and hope to die*! It's all promises, vows, extravagant protests. God is their witness – for want of anyone else to blame! Or they'll swear on their own son's head – especially if he's no longer a minor! At the end of a quarrel they murmur breathlessly as they bend you back across the bed: 'There now, doesn't *that* prove I love you?'

"They'll *all* love you sincerely, Joy dear, provided you don't go too far! Never overstep the mark, you're only in the supporting role and you'll never play the lead. They never do desert the little woman who waits for them – in a house with kids sleeping inside ..."

I shrugged blithely as if to imply that she couldn't really be serious, and was exaggerating, of course. Surely the poor dear couldn't mean it?

"You're not the marrying kind, Joy my love!"

That comment really struck home. It was a final judgement, a jinx mother had cast on me. Joy-my-love – three well-worn little words that dance in front of my eyes: written

14

in red ink, in felt-pen, on crumpled telegrams or tear-stained farewell notes. Three bloody silly little words which leap off all those presents I refused and which adorn those I longed for but never received. I'd need a large suitcase to store all the Joy-my-loves offered me. What's more, if I had it, I'd rifle through it feverishly, like an amnesiac hunting for that single Joy-my-love which was missing. That phrase never uttered, written, exclaimed or groaned. *He* never once called me Joy-my-love, and that is what hurts and obsesses me: to him I was just Joy and today I'm no longer even that.

I let myself drift, flinging myself into different experiences and sensations; dwelling on the past yet always on the run, always watching and listening – for a door, a voice or a taxi arriving at night. For a while I was carried along on a tidal wave of friends, lovers and acquaintances, some close and some not so close. Cushioned by them I lived for the moment, surrendering to random demands and fleeting pleasures. When I grew bored, like a ghost I was quick to revisit the familiar scenes of my own special tragedy: a dark gleaming avenue; the rainy town of Nantes, where his window used to shine at night; the front room of a particular local *bistro*; an hotel's pink neon sign; the cavernous car park that provided somewhere to make love in case of emergency; a white placard advertising that Apartment To Let, in which we will never live.

But despite all such wishful thinking I would return home, double-lock the door and throw myself upon the bed, burying my head beneath the pillow so as not to hear his voice any more nor to remember his mannerisms. As when, for example, he would abruptly stop talking in order to drag me to him. ... Or the way he would rub against my body, making me cry sometimes when entering me brutally. On those occasions he hurt me and would deliberately continue doing so, withdrawing from me without saying even one word. Marc Charroux, swine and bastard, take it out on yourself if you're so tough. He never would say anything, though. Never a whisper, not even a cliché, nor the faintest Joy-my-love.

15

CHAPTER TWO

I would turn the pages of my small notebook, my Bible filled with names and numbers of friends, relations – and lovers.

I hated my night-time partners, they were just strangers in the night, passing ships departing unmourned. In those days Joy asked only to be taken away to some unfamiliar beach before surrendering. Passion somehow seemed stimulated by good weather, different food and nothing else to do but bask in the sun by day and make love by night. Returning home was always dismal, however, suitcases seemed even heavier to carry, filled as they were with dirty washing and trashy souvenirs. It took only a 'See you soon', which was really a definitive 'Goodbye', to bleach my tan as the rain fell on the taxi rank. The end of even the most wretched escapade represents a race against the clock: whoever leaves first, wins. Like a fool I always left it just that bit too late and so, having given the other, craftier games-player time to tell me where to get off, I'd lose – and the whole business would start all over again. Another humiliating flight with those suitcases crammed with rubbish. Another search for somewhere to take refuge and recover. And waiting – the interminable waiting.

I would gaze half-expectantly at the faces of hurrying passers-by, as if seeking some proof in a smile or a look – proof that to all these hateful impassive males I still existed. I wanted to go further, faster, to save time yet still find what I was searching for.

I tried everything – I was borne along on a tide of passion. I needed love. I was ready for anything. I'd have happily devoted my life to just one man, but it was the other sort I attracted. The silent, over-polite ones gravitated around me, insidious men who would sit at my table, coldly and deliberately looking me up and down. They taught me that the unattached woman is a whore: she awaits the client knowing that in return for a modicum of tenderness she will have to give rather too much. Their masculine presumption revolted me.

They would talk to me as if I were a halfwitted child, greedily sizing me up in the process. They would assess the curve of my buttocks, calculate the firmness of my breasts. Faced with such leering lechery I would slip away quickly, preserving my illusions and trying to escape from those gross, threatening contacts. Isolated because of my hesitant refusals, I would withdraw myself slowly from the city and its pressures.

I used to shut myself in my jasmine-scented room and there, tense and depressed, would masturbate for hours on end, searching endlessly for the orgasm which would banish my obsession like some tidal wave. I measured the passage of time by the play of shadows across the ceiling. Lying in back-breaking positions over the edge of the bed, with my head buried in cushions, I worked desperately on my body. I knew its every weakness and did my utmost to torture myself cruelly.

I knew exactly how to tease my nipples to an unbearable pitch, and I would rub the soft flesh of my inner thighs against the nap of the bed cover until my cunt wept with pleasure. I was intoxicated with its bitter-sweet scents, with the musky lingering odour which clung to my fingers like an essence of pink and mauve flowers, a heady unguent falling droplet by droplet upon the embroidered sheets between which I thrashed and squirmed.

This twin quest for love and satisfaction preoccupied me for years. I had for so long been in the habit of masturbating that the act had become an indispensable function, a need so deep that I would never dream of resisting it. I had strong urges to touch my body and I simply had to satisfy them instantly. I would undo my nightdress and slide a hand across

17

my swollen breasts or, through my skirt, very lightly press two fingers over the opening of my sex – by this casual contact achieving the same overwhelming sensation which the firmer, more peremptory feel of a strange hand might have provoked.

I was in love with myself. In the evening I would delay the moment of self-surrender as long as possible, I would struggle to control the spasms of pleasure which racked my whole body. I employed the methods which would make me shudder and tremble – lengthy leisurely caresses, the very delicate scratch of a fingernail upon the clitoris itself. I would twist my limbs, contort myself in all kinds of outrageous positions, almost to the point of inflicting pain, yet without being able to admire my own poses or see what I was so lewdly offering. I revelled in exaggerating these abandoned postures I adopted and in the copiousness of the slick trickle that oozed between my thighs. My fantasies became ever more involved and unbearable. I would pummel and punch my body and drive myself to the point of no return, almost in awe of the violence of the paroxysm which would leave me in a state of collapse.

Day by day I would spend even more time alone, satisfying this craving for myself. It was the best time of my life because I never deceived myself.

I met him during one of these carnal retreats of mine. It was four years ago but I still remember that encounter so well that I can recreate its smallest detail. That August 18th we had attended the funeral of an uncle from the provinces. The burial was taking place in a quiet corner of Père Lachaise. An oppressively hot sun beat down on the few mourners who had cut short their summer holidays and braved the heat to pay their last respects to Gaspard Tulard. He was mother's uncle and I'd never met him, but his name had haunted my childhood. As long as I can remember, the grim warning had been issued: "If you don't behave yourself, I'll send you away to stay with Uncle Gaspard!''

I associated Uncle Gaspard with the big bad wolf; he loomed large in my youthful consciousness like some cruel and hideous monster. I only uncovered that hateful lie many years later. Mother was tidying up at the time, sorting through a photograph album, and as she flicked its pages, happened to exclaim: ''That's Uncle Gaspard.''

Poor Gaspard Tulard: for years I'd imagined him as horned and hunchbacked, devouring small children and plunging whole families into despair. In fact, Uncle Gaspard was not like that at all. He had a broad forehead under his thinning hair and, as seemed obligatory in old photos, his paunch jutted proudly. In this faded photograph he appeared sad and mysterious. His black topcoat was immaculately cut, he wore pinstriped trousers and his bootees shone against the Persian rug.

His expression was fascinating, it was so penetrating that I felt almost dizzy and so suggestive it made me feel ill at ease. While I lingered over this photo, mother approached and murmured as she stood beside me:

''Quite a character, Uncle Gaspard. He was the pride and the black sheep of the family. He was the first one in the whole region to own a motor car and everybody would watch the family go off for the Sunday morning drive ... Black sheep too, because one day, on the way back home from his usual bar, where he always drank with his childhood cronies, he had a crazy impulse. He opened a brothel. True, he was a bachelor, but all the same ...''

Gaspard Tulard, brothel-keeper. In fact he wasn't too involved with its running, but that was his way of providing for his common-law wife, 'Aunt' Germaine. So he set her up in a nice house of her own on the outskirts of Limoges. He divided his life between Limoges and Paris where the more serious textile business occupied him. One morning he died in bed, calling out for Germaine. During his last months Gaspard went a little senile, unable to remember that Germaine had been dead for years and his brothel in Limoges had been closed down.

He'd never wanted to sell it, however, and the 'hotel' crumbled slowly amid the new suburban developments which mushroomed around it.

One day I stopped off to visit the place. Opening the front door I entered the darkened parlour where strips of purple and gold wallpaper hung down in tatters. Vanished furniture had left its imprint against the walls. You could picture the heavy wardrobes, well-waxed tables, and huge beds in which wicked uncle's tenants slept. A dusty cheval-glass concealed forgotten revels under its silvering, and idly I imagined the plump buttocks of some country girl heaving in response to the furious assault of a tipsy customer. When I left I felt as if I were closing a door on that bygone world, a nocturnal paradise where women awaited men while chatting together in the parlour, clad in silks which disguised yet flattered their buxom figures. I regretted not having been able, just once, to mingle with them and wait to be chosen too ...

The coffin descended into the dry earth. Mother fanned herself with a listless hand. I turned towards the silent silhouettes and then I saw him.

He wore a lightweight suit and had his hands in his pockets. He was gazing intently at me, his stare not in the least ingratiating. He was looking me over coolly and this suggestive scrutiny made me feel uneasy. I leaned forward very slightly, pretending to be engrossed in looking at the open grave, and turned once again towards him. He was still staring. I told myself that he had a sort of raffish charm: I felt like telling him to leave us alone with our thoughts, funerals weren't laid on for his entertainment. Actually I liked his tan and good looks. Mother leaned across to remark:

"Joy, we're being stared at."

I was not sure whether she was referring to him or to members of the family, who were mostly sniffling and mopping their brows. The priest turned towards us. He too was looking at me. At that moment everyone seemed to be doing just that, just then. I became very conscious of the urgent murmur of the prayers. I felt thoroughly ashamed. An irresistible compulsion was urging me to go across to the man and talk to him. Confused thoughts whirled through my mind and I attributed these to the heat. I wanted to caress myself, to pull my panties slowly down my thighs and challenge that detestable man. I was shaking at the knees.

"Aren't you feeling well?" mother asked.

"I'm going in the shade," I replied.

I left the main group and leaned against a tree. When I turned round again he had disappeared. I scanned the mass of crosses and gravestones and caught sight of him some distance away, making for the gate. Immediately I headed in the same direction, abandoning mother and Uncle Gaspard without a second thought. I wanted this man. I had to have him.

The heat was overpowering. I was sweating and my black dress clung uncomfortably to my body. I began to run. A woman with a vase of pale flowers watched me disapprovingly. By the main entrance to the cemetery various passers-by were strolling. I ignored the odd looks they gave me.

He had stopped by a black car and was inside before I could reach it. When he saw me, a wicked grin came over his face and he motioned to me slyly. This mocking little signal mortified me. He had understood what I wanted and was enjoying his triumph – his double triumph, for he was driving away slowly, looking straight at me as he did so. The message was unmistakable: "I don't like women who make the running."

I had never felt so insulted. The black car squeezed between two buses and vanished. I turned back towards the cemetery, humiliated and angry, appalled at the thought of never seeing him again. I got lost, in fact, wandering down long straight pathways where the unbearable heat wafted aloft the scent of withered flowers. Behind one mausoleum I discerned a shadowy outline hiding beside a black marble cross. I slowed down as I passed and found myself opposite a tall, nice-looking curlyheaded guy who was observing me worriedly. Like a fool, I thought he was ill – sunstroke perhaps – and went up to him, all polite and concerned and ready to help. I even put on my glasses.

"Are you unwell? Do you need any help?"

The tall fellow gazed at me with some surprise, then looked down. I followed his glance and caught sight of his prick protruding from his jeans: he was in fact masturbating violently. I stepped back, but only in order to get a better view of what was on display. He accelerated his rhythm and looked imploringly at me. I shook my head sadly, but stayed there, why I don't know, until the end, when he unburdened himself, whimpering like a child, yet with such force that the bottom of my black dress received the tribute of his pleasure. He stayed where he was, quite close to me, his hand gripping his prick, obviously keen to know what reactions his exhibition had provoked.

I wanted to speak to him, to explain that I too had urges just like his own – the irresistible need to be watched, for example – and that I used to dream of whole coachloads of silent men compelled to watch me without being able to make the slightest movement. I would have confessed to him that every evening I too masturbated, and that I too understood. But I said nothing, murmuring only:

"It's a pity ..."

Then I went back, giving him a wry smile of helpless complicity and he remained there leaning against the tomb with his hand still clutching himself, unhappy and disappointed.

Mother and I drove home in a black limousine. Gaspard Tulard had planned his funeral rites to the last detail: this included the menu for the lunch party, the transport arrangements, and all the farewell gifts. Everyone accompanying him to the cemetery received a black package tied with black ribbon. Mine contained a card and a key. The card read: *My dear little girl, I know you are beautiful and I've loved you for so long. Don't lose this key to a priceless treasure, a secret I've never told anybody about and which I keep for you.*

That evening mother returned to Geneva.

I had dinner with Irina and Margo, two girls I'm really fond of. I guzzled various sugary concoctions, downed a quantity of mixed drinks and nibbled at all sorts of exotic fruits. I was well away, but Margo dragged me along to the '78', where she had to go to meet the usual crowd of male admirers eager for her favours.

Margo is stunning. A tall supple blonde, lean and muscular as a foal. She has long legs, small breasts and little buttocks round as apples. She is attractive and knows it, leading whoever is chasing her a merry dance. When she has drunk too much she makes up to me outrageously and endlessly nuzzles my ears, whispering horrendous sweet talk and nonsense which makes me laugh and quiver simultaneously. This sort of thing: "Joy my love, say yes, give in to me, surrender your lovely self, you'll be my prisoner, I'll punish you as cruelly as I can, I'll ravish you, you'll beg for mercy but I won't take pity on you, I'll make you die, die happy you hear, Joy darling, Joy my love …"

She kissed me full on the lips, her own lips burning. I liked that kiss. I had the feeling I was being watched, which excited me all the more and I kissed Margo back, passionately. When I opened my eyes I saw him, standing there in front of me. Hands in pockets, he was smiling at me teasingly, while Margo clasped my hand very tightly in hers.

CHAPTER THREE

The surging throng inside the '78' swirled around us. Margo leaned over to Irina and fell deep in conversation with her. He advanced, holding out a hand.

"My name's Marc. I know all about you. Come with me."

The grotesque macho line, evidently. My dazed look was intended partly to side-track him, as I was shaking my head to try to convey the fact that I didn't even know him.

"I've been thinking of you ever since this morning, Joy. I've looked all over Paris for you. I knew I'd find you. Come on."

As soon as his hand touched mine I abandoned all resistance and let myself be guided towards the exit. For a moment we remained motionless in the lukewarm air of the Champs Elysées. Marc was gazing intently at me.

"You're not just attractive. It's not as easy as that, worse luck."

I regained my composure, managing a smile, and waited for the inevitable phrases, the single mistake which would put me off completely.

"What do you get out of these places? They're always the same, night after night, same dramas same loneliness. What are you searching for? I didn't imagine you as one of a crowd. You seemed so isolated, solitary, distanced from people, yet once again I find you in the worst sort of company."

I made no reply and adopted an expression of annoyance.

"I'm sorry. I wanted to talk to you but didn't know what to say. I'll see you home."

He walked off peevishly and opened the door of his black car.

"Get in."

I did so, rather tensely and warily. I'd sobered up all of a sudden. He gunned the engine and drove off crazily with tyres squealing. His face was set and he stared stonily ahead as if I didn't exist. I realized with amazement that he was taking the shortest route back to my place.

"How do you know my address?" I asked him dolefully.

He smiled but did not answer, nor did he say a word until we stopped at my door. He bent over and kissed my hand. Then he looked at me gravely.

"I'll be waiting."

He opened the door my side, accompanied me as far as the hallway, where he immediately switched on the minute-light and then left. I saw him go back to sit in the car, where he lit a cigarette.

Somewhat reluctantly I took the lift up to the silent flat full of my fantasies. I flung my bag on to the armchair, began to undress and then, unable to resist, rushed to the window. The black car was still there and cigarette smoke drifted from the nearside window up into the night. I was disarmed and flustered, but melting with pleasure and almost won over. I took the longest, most luxurious and scented bath of my life. Then I did my hair and took off my make-up with exaggerated deliberation before dashing yet again to the window. He was still there. I slid between the clean sheets and tossed and turned a while to find the best position, glancing anxiously at the hands of the alarm clock now moving towards morning.

At three a.m. he was still there, and the small black car hadn't moved. I didn't deserve such treatment. I slipped on a shirt and jeans, hammered at the door of the lift which was slow to work, and marched determinedly across to the car, pulling the driver's door open viciously.

"Look here, that's quite enough. Either you go or come on up."

His eyes were red and swollen like a spaniel's.

"Thank you, Joy."

He followed me slowly, giving me little glances which made

me uncomfortable because by now I was scared that things would not turn out well.

My heart was full of wild expectation, but I was dreading that first half-hour of hesitations, awkward banter and sidelong looks. I did not want him to spoil things by some clumsiness or other and ruin the moment I'd been waiting for.

I felt that if I did not take the initiative at once, he would compliment me on the colour of the upholstery or find my flat perfectly delightful. So I threw my keys on a chair and undid my watch (I hate wearing a wristwatch during sex). Then I abruptly pulled off my sweater, messing up my hair in the process. I unfastened my jeans and tugged them down as far as my ankles, along with my panties. I stood there, immobile, purposely ignoring him. His gaze gave me gooseflesh.

He stared at me, murmuring: "My God, you're so lovely!" Then he walked across and seemed to take an hour before touching my breasts. The moment he did, I knew it was special. In order to cut short any conversation, I lay down on the bed, spreading my thighs so he could see my whole pubic region and how ready I was. He took his time and I had to control myself and remain patient while he removed his clothes. Men are rarely graceful when undressing: they are awkward if not downright clumsy.

When he laid his hand against the small of my back, one of my most sensitive areas, I let out a gasp. His nails teasingly brushed the skin as he stroked me with his fingertips, moving infinitely slowly from the cleft of my buttocks to the very edge of my vagina. Well aware of how he was tormenting me he stopped at the brink, as it were, and paid no heed to my writhing motions. After a slight pause he began again.

The unbearable caresses worked up to my shoulders. It seemed he had an unerring instinct for detecting my most sensitive areas. I was trembling by the time his hands returned once more to the soft satin flesh of my belly after pausing briefly at my hips and bush – which by now was indeed burning. He repeated this sequence a score of times and I bit my lip in order not to scream. Then his other hand concentrated upon my breasts, nails tickling, scratching and finally pinching both nipples.

I felt myself succumb to a series of shudders of pleasure and I shifted position so he could no longer avoid my aching sex. His fingers penetrated me and worked in a slow to-and-fro rhythm until I uttered my first cry. I wanted to push him away but he now resumed, using his mouth, and I no longer had strength to resist. He was doing whatever he wanted to, taking me almost to climax before stopping abruptly. Whenever I temporarily regained control of myself he continued to assert his domination, causing me some discomfort.

I was seized by a form of nervous trembling – then he pulled back. I managed to breathe properly again and was momentarily overcome by a sensation of simultaneous heat and cold.

When he finally entered me he sank deep inside and remained there without moving. He forced back my head by pulling my hair and made me look him straight in the eyes: only then did he start to undulate his hips. With each thrust I groaned, but his rhythm continued slow and I needed to go faster. I grabbed at his limbs, ripped his half-open shirt and clasped him ever more tightly. I pinched his skin and pressed myself avidly against his body hair. But as soon as he sensed that I was overtaking him and nearing climax he would freeze, stay buried to the hilt inside me, mocking me with his control. Suddenly he delivered an incredibly violent thrust which almost gave me a heart attack and followed it with another and another. I bit my knuckles, crying, then I came like a crazy woman, yelling words of love at him which I had never uttered before to anyone. Finally I collapsed in a heap, choking with pleasure. He pulled out of me roughly, rubbing his penis against my trembling belly. I was horrified when I realized what he intended, and begged him hoarsely: "Inside me, *please* come inside ..."

He stared straight into my eyes and spattered me with his semen as if spitting out an insult. He had not shared pleasure with me but had taken it for himself. I hated him and his contempt made me feel ashamed. I had so wanted him to flood my very depths: my body had been thirsting for precisely that. My head throbbed and I felt cheated and defeated. My heart hammered at my ribcage and when, after a very long time, I finally sat up dishevelled and degraded, I saw him leaving, without a word. He shut the door behind him and I stayed where I was, absolutely aghast, so sick with shame that I wanted to die. I didn't believe that he could depart like that, without so much as a glance at the wretched creature huddled on the bed.

I could not bear being abandoned in such a way, and at dawn, drenched by the icy rain trickling down my neck, I was wandering the glistening, slippery streets. I found myself heading for Margo's place.

Heavy smoke billowed out as the door opened. She was drunk and the flat was full of people lounging around in the murk. The place reeked, exuding that stale small-hours atmosphere of exhaustion. Margo planted a lengthy kiss on my lips.

"You're trembling darling, you must be cold. Well I'll keep you warm, you sweet little piece, come into my parlour and I'll gobble you up ..."

I thrust her away in irritation and pushed into the darkened room. Suggestive chuckles from the shadows greeted my arrival, while hands groped me as I passed, brushing against my breasts and trying to feel me just where I was most numb and most afflicted by disgust. Unrecognizable voices called out to me.

"Hello Joy – looking for me then, sweetheart?"

I heard all sorts of whispered, suggestive comments, and crude remarks were made accompanied by nasty sniggers. Someone drew me down on to the cushioned softness of a sofa; it engulfed me in slow motion. I felt as if I were drowning in a calm sea. Margo had found me again and sidled up to me.

"Drink this, Joy my sweet, and drown your sorrows."

Margo's gushing persistence was intolerable. I drained a heavy and rather rough liqueur at one gulp and heard something whispered in my ear which at first I didn't understand.

"You naughty little bitch, I know why you came here, just let yourself go ..."

The anonymous conversationalist began to push my sweater up over my aching breasts. He began to massage them in leisurely fashion, concentrating on stimulating the nipples which were very far from erect. To my surprise I arched backwards, beginning to savour this furtive excitation. I undid my jeans myself, impatient to feel those relentless fingers which I knew must soon forage my flesh.

The darkness was so complete that I could not distinguish my shadowy handler. The man's rough digits found my once again sensitive sex and then slithered to the rear orifice, gently parting its puckered portals. Lightly, almost imperceptibly, his finger sank in. It worked deeper still and I twisted to one side to facilitate its progress. The finger turned slowly within me as if to enlarge its domain.

His mouth moved moistly over my breasts and then past my hips until it reached my distended clitoris, and meanwhile that finger worked faster and faster. Powerless to resist, I had two acute spasms of pleasure. The mouth, soaking now, returned to my face. Someone started to laugh. A match flared, dispelling the darkness for a moment. Margo was weeping noiselessly. I hurriedly dressed and slunk towards the front door.

Out of the silence somewhere in my wake that mocking voice intercepted me: "Bye bye Joy, you sexy little slut!"

CHAPTER FOUR

Mother only wanted to visit our large and beautiful house in the Dordogne during the summer holidays. It was there that I began to learn about boys. Each year on our arrival elegant white-clad youths came and strutted below our windows. I would run down the stairs and hurl myself into their arms, excited at seeing them again and finding them taller, older, sometimes even bearded. They too seemed fascinated by my physical development over the past year and would blurt out compliments. I shimmied amongst them so they could admire my cheekily short new dress, displaying my bony knees and slender thighs with all the assurance of an experienced vamp.

Around the middle of August the weather would break: heavy storms would herald long weeks of rain. That was when we would organize endless card games in the sitting-room where the first open fire of the season blazed. Our young companions were good, stoical losers, which was as well because, with my mother's connivance, I used to cheat.

It was not unusual for me to feel a foot brush against my long bare leg – and I would pretend to concentrate deeply upon my next move. I'd give the person opposite me meaningful looks for I took these attentions as proofs of friendship. I smiled in the way I had practised before my hand-mirror, with my head thrust forwards slightly, one finger to my lips. I then responded to the teasing tickle with less discreet pressures. My mother would by then be pulling a superior face, or occasionally betraying her irritation, and I'd feel the friendly leg move away from mine while signs of acute confusion would appear upon the other player's face.

On those rare days when the sun dispersed the cloud we – mother, our friends and myself – would go swimming in the Dordogne. We'd walk over shingle to an isolated creek and there we would take off our clothes, under which we wore skimpy bathing costumes. I must admit that on those occasions I was jealous of my mother. The boys shamelessly ogled her athletic yet voluptuous older woman's body.

Their lingering looks at her full-breasted figure were casually affected, but she had only to turn away from the youths for them to exchange knowing glances behind her back. They gazed in awe at her strong, suntanned hips and her firm, rounded buttocks which were accentuated by her tight swimsuit.

Unable to rival mother's charms, I resorted to daring in order to divert the adolescents' attentions back to myself. I would turn sullen, pout and sigh and stretch out languorously upon the beach mat. I always carefully spread my legs to allow that fine blonde down now sparsely adorning my pubis to protrude from either side of my minuscule briefs. Again I became the focus of attention: pebbles and drops of cold water were lobbed at me and I would close my eyes, secure in the delicious certainty of having a wonderful vacation.

The most important event of the summer took place at the end of August. That was the village fair. Every year the same fairground buskers returned to set up their roundabouts in the main square. Lazy holidaymakers thronged to this show, which of course, was despised by the natives. The nasal tones of loudspeaker systems and the aroma of candy floss disturbed the peace of the village, while the unusual volume of traffic disturbed the small town.

I was fifteen when my mother allowed me to go the fair alone for the first time. We happened to be in the garden, busy picking flowers, and the night was drawing in. Mother took my arm.

"You're fifteen," she said. "This year I feel too ancient for gadding around fairground dodgems and stalls all night. You'll go on your own, won't you? You're grown up now, Joy my love, you don't need me there. Christine or Sophie will go with you. Only you must promise me you won't be back too late. Is that all right?"

I remained silent. For a long time I had known that on the evening of the fair the older girls would go along to dance with boys, and that afterwards they certainly did not return straight home. Small girls told each other unbelievably fevered stories about steamy encounters in the grass of the fairground enclosure. So – it was to be at the age of fifteen that *it* would happen! I kissed my mother, promising her to be home on the stroke of midnight like Cinderella, to be as good as a first Communicant, and not to speak to boys I didn't know, nor to drink anything except grenadine and lemonade.

For two days I rummaged through my suitcases hunting for appropriate apparel for such an occasion. Finally I chose a front-fastening white dress with three buttons which I had the definite intention of undoing immediately I was out of the house.

At about five p.m. on the great day I lounged in a long, ritualistic bath, floating luxuriously in the old-fashioned tub and toying with my breasts which bobbed saucily above the foam. The bath emptied to reveal my sun-bronzed body dripping like a rock at low tide. I examined my flat stomach, still skinny thighs, and the curly thatch now growing more thickly between them. That was the first time I dared put a finger into my dormant sex and I_closed my legs again as violently as if I had received an electric shock. I stood up and left the bathroom trembling, after drenching myself in toilet water as sickly and scented as an English boiled sweet.

That evening I did not keep my promises. I drank chilled white wine, smoked filter tipped cigarettes, and kissed Bertrand behind the dance marquee. Midnight found me sticky-mouthed and glassy-eyed in a 2CV which was jolting up an interminable hill. The night was pitch-black. Suddenly Bertrand stopped by a small side road. I stiffened, thinking that the moment had come. I'm not sure of course exactly when this occurred, but I recall concentrating on the winding road ahead as if it would reveal that fantastic mystery I so dreaded.

Bertrand leaned across, stammering "Joy my love" several times, and tried to kiss me. In fact this was a difficult undertaking. I stubbornly refused to part my lips, for fear that he would introduce not simply his tongue but an extra element of lewd abandon. He nibbled endlessly at my ears, throat, and nape, managing despite himself to crease my pretty white dress by palping my large breasts which both fascinated and intimidated him. He smelt of lavender, perspiration and white wine, but I tried hard to view him as attractive, even opening my legs in order to facilitate his clumsy caresses. When he had overcome the damp and tricky obstacle of my lace panties, he emitted awe-inspiring groans and his shaking fingers roved dementedly over my moist mound, trying to force themselves still further into its folds and hollows. I was breathing heavily, eager to anticipate sensations not yet in evidence, and increasingly nervous and disappointed. Bertrand took advantage of this to place my free hand on his hard upright prick which he had surreptitiously extracted from his fawn linen trousers.

My fingers closed round this long hot object, while I half expected lightning to strike me: my life would surely never again be the same! Without realizing it, I instinctively discovered and employed that basic motion nobody had ever taught me: as I adopted it I stared fascinated at the brownish stem thrusting between my slim fingers and, awe-struck, heard Bertrand's ever more dramatic moans. I held him tighter, jerked him faster, and he began gasping: "Joy my love, Joy my love!"

I slid my other hand as quietly as I could beneath my white dress and caressed my stomach and pubis, which were quivering in rhythm with my other hand's movements. The interior of my vagina felt unusually hot, a little as if I were bleeding. And the moment I managed to insert a finger inside myself, I saw stars – while almost simultaneously Bertrand ejaculated into my hand. I did not move. My eyes were wide open and I was in a state of suspended animation and shock. The palm of my hand was all sticky and I was anxiously wondering if I had hurt him and, even more important, what to do next.

I do not think I've ever felt such intense pleasure as Bertrand unwittingly gave me. Every evening until the end of that summer I sought him out in his 2CV. Then, patiently, he would teach me to caress his sex, or more specifically to put it into my mouth, deeper and deeper, then to move my lips gently and much later to work on him with my tongue. For the first time I sucked him to his climax that way, and I acquired what might be called the taste for it: fellation intoxicated me and I loved that sensation of slight nausea which inexplicably gave me both a thirst and an orgasm. On the last day of the holidays he laid me down on the grass and took my virginity. I felt nothing, apart from pain, and by way of exacting revenge I insisted on taking his prick in my mouth afterwards so that he could make his usual contribution.

Although all the men I've had since have given me pleasure in their different ways, I've never again experienced the powerful sensations and deep feelings I shared with Bertrand. Marc was to destroy all that: he ransacked that first happiness, my youth, while forcing upon me a sensual fulfilment I had never suspected.

After that louse broke into my life like a burglar, in the summer holidays I used to wander through a Paris that was half-deserted. I was like a lost soul, feeble and prematurely gone to seed. Sometimes I'd stop on a street corner and bury my head in my hands, unable to understand why he had behaved as he did. I had asked nothing of him and had never harmed him in any way. I was living quite peacefully until he came along and destroyed that peace. The days were endless and the nights even worse. I exhausted myself thinking about him, reliving unforgettable moments of pleasure and pain.

Mother was in Greece and I was alone, an orphan with no one to talk to, and broke. I don't know why it is, but I never have money when I need it, and whenever I do have it, it disappears as fast as Marc. I had only Margo to help me. I paid her a surprise visit and found her sober, without make-up and pretty as a picture. Margo, my old schoolfriend, with whom I'd shared everything in the days when we'd nothing to share. My evil genius who persuaded me into 'posing for photos' to earn a crust. Margo my best and only friend who stole my men and passed on her lovers ... I told her about Marc and she took me into her arms, murmuring endearments. Suddenly she hesitated.

"Tell me, was I really very smashed the other night?"

I replied that she was indeed, she'd annoyed me and I'd been cross with her. A large tear trickled down one cheek as she apologized.

"You mustn't be angry with me. There are times I just don't know what I'm doing any more ..."

I told her I never bore her a grudge, and that it wasn't important anyhow. I also mentioned I could use a loan. She pulled a face at that.

"Darling I'm cleaned out. I don't have a cent and tomorrow morning I'm off to Los Angeles with David. Yes, you know, *that* David. So you see how things are, I have to leave with that exasperating guy, just to survive – because I can't even pay my rent for the month. But it's different for you, you can always sell some photos."

I told her I needed money right away and besides, photographers always took an eternity to pay. She looked dumbfounded.

"I do have one solution, but you'd never –"

"I can't be choosy, you realize."

"Not too marvellous a solution, I know, but it's bailed out quite a few girls. There's this amateur photographer ... All you need do is pose, photos only. He's very proper, though he isn't always on his own: if there *are* one or two others there too, not to worry, they won't touch. He pays 2000 francs per session."

"You're crazy. I'm known, I can't possibly pose for that kind of photo. The model agencies and magazines would recognize me and – no it's madness."

"But my love, he takes these photos for his own pleasure. There's never any problem."

I left, telling her I'd think about it. That evening I was obliged to accept the offer. Deep down I know that what persuaded me to agree was that sneaking obsession with showing myself off, which always excites me more than anything else. I also knew the escapade might well turn out to be dangerous: this in itself made me want to sink to the level of this sleazy set-up.

I have never revealed to anyone what happened on that occasion. Now I am writing about it in this book, thousands of men and women will discover my secret. In fact that pleases me, for it's another way of posing – and of exposing myself. Since this adventure numerous magazines have published model shots of me, always dressed (more or less) rather than nude. Yet no one who writes me fan letters, imagining I'm as respectable as I am blonde – not to mention inaccessible, difficult to approach, distant, chic and so on – ever suspects that I've posed for blue photos, or that I actually enjoyed that sordid exhibition and took pleasure in participating. Since I met Marc I deliberately went to the limits of the acceptable, experiencing a morbid excitement in my sexual degradation which never allowed me rest.

Margo was afraid I'd change my mind at the last minute, which is probably why she took it upon herself to come along with me. She drove us there in David's vast car. David himself was no great lover: he was weak, superficial, charmless, vulgar and corrupt, but he did have introductions and contacts on every level of Parisian society. For Margo, David was a sort of travel agency, an exclusive club, a credit account at all the boutiques on the Avenue Victor Hugo and the Faubourg St Honoré, a guaranteed fortnight of winter sports at Crans-sur-Sierre, a villa with swimming pool on Ibiza, the inevitable trip to L.A. returning via New York. In return for these privileges and a regularly topped-up account with the Jordanian Bank, Margo was completely at David's beck and call.

"You've got yourself the worst bargain in Paris," I couldn't

36

help remarking to her while she was driving flat out in that flashy and appalling limousine.

"For God's sake don't say that! Joy my love, don't I just know it, but I'll soon be thirty ...'

"In five years' time, you fool. You've got some way to go yet ..."

"But Joy, thirty means the end. It's death. You can't go out any more. How *ghastly*."

"I think you're crazy!" I almost yelled at her. She saw how annoyed I was and said nothing else during the rest of that long drive.

I was wearing a tight black sheath dress which a mere two buttons would open, but nothing underneath.

I don't remember exactly when we turned off the autoroute and found ourselves deep in the country. We drove through a forest and stopped at last outside a large white house, the sort owned by doctors and lawyers on the outskirts of provincial towns. The ground-floor rooms were lit and a reddish glow was visible through curtains not fully drawn. Margo, her eyes sparkling, rang the front-door bell.

"I want to stay and watch."

A young fairhaired woman opened the door. For a moment she looked us coolly up and down then, still silent, ushered us into a sitting-room furnished in crimson velvet. A heady musky incense permeated the enormous room whose walls, carpet and lacquered furniture were all of an identical blood-red. An icebucket with an open champagne bottle stood on one table. In the centre of the room spotlights concealed in the rafters illuminated a gynaecological examination chair which gleamed forbiddingly.

"There we are," Margo murmured, taking my hand. "Are you ready?"

My heart was palpitating. I hardly dared utter a word. I had to control myself in order not to undress at once and climb on to that armchair where I could lie completely open. Margo offered me a glass of champagne which I drank at one gulp. She stroked my cheek.

"Now you must undress."

I unfastened the two buttons and my dress fell to the carpet. I remained standing there, passive and moist, until Margo pushed me towards the chair.

"Get into it. He'll be here soon."

The moment I was installed in the chair I felt dizzy. The seat's position had been carefully angled. It was back-breaking, and when I slid my feet into the metal stirrups I felt my abdomen thrust forward so that the whole area of my loins was completely exposed. I was spread so wide that my thighs quivered. I remained motionless, blinded by the spotlights, and in this shameful and exciting pose I felt my labia part and slowly open. Margo caressed my breasts.

"I knew you would like this. My God, you're sublime," she breathed. "You look as though you'll split apart like that ... He puts something in the champagne, you realize. Perhaps that's why you're so wet down there ..."

Just then the door opened and a man walked over to me. I'm sure my heartbeats must have been audible the other side of the house. My hands were trembling. My thighs and pubis were bathed in an ice-cold sweat.

"Excellent, excellent," the man said loudly. It seemed to free me from the spell. "My compliments, darling, your friend is superb," he was saying to Margo," we'll be able to work together."

I caught sight of him adjusting a mounted camera so that it was pointing at me.

"You'll be able to vary the quality of the picture, my dear. To see yourself in detail, as you have surely never seen yourself before ..."

He pressed a button and a huge screen appeared. A grey indistinct image wavered then leaped into focus. My cunt became clearly recognizable in a vast, obscene close-up. Blown up out of all proportion, the picture showed a pink sculpture shading into the darkness of a mauve abyss. Up there on the screen a shining growth pulsed like a living flower ... The man delivered a dispassionate commentary on what he was observing:

"The vagina is wide open, labia not too large. Yes, it's really magnificent."

He tilted the camera towards my buttocks. The cleft revealed its pursed star twinkling gently.

"Relax please, relax the muscles."

In amazement I saw my flesh open and tremble slightly.

"Don't move any more."

The screen continued recording my body's secrets, then a series of clicking shutters informed me that a special electronic camera was being used. The door opened and a second man entered.

"Ah, here you are," exclaimed the camera operator. "You see, my dear friend, that the attraction of youthful sex organs lies in the soft colouring. Take a look at that pearly pink, the ochre pallor of the epidermis. Rare indeed. Everything here is tender, glowing, velvety, with the mucous membranes remarkably firm, while the copiousness of secretion in the present case is exceptional."

The stares I knew were being directed at the very depths of myself acted as the subtlest, most irresistible of caresses. My narcissism revelled in them and my enforced indecency of posture was provoking an almost painful excitement. The sexual emotion I was feeling emanated from myself through the medium of these two men who were looking at but not touching me.

"For your initiation you have a small degree of latitude. This girl is wonderful and healthy, which is relatively rare. Soon you'll see all the masterpieces in my collection. Some of them are extraordinary."

"What an amazing fixation. I must admit the experience is surprising," the new arrival commented hoarsely. "But do you derive complete satisfaction like this?"

"Look, my friend, what matters is that the model needs to display herself. Only this way do I have at my disposal the ideal partner. Our relationship is established through the camera and both of us have only this one desire. Some real failures come here sometimes, girls who submit to the test solely out of desperation. For the thorough-going exhibitionist such an opportunity can become a true deliverance. I make exhibitionism possible on the most impersonal level: the motive, I mean, has to be absolutely pure. The desire for display. Nothing else. Alas, authentic cases are rare. I can spot the fakers who come here just for the money, or the tyros who get uptight the moment the ah, bourgeois, limits of the exhibition are exceeded.

"The most interesting case history in my experience is that of a celebrated young actress you'll no doubt have seen and admired in various movies. This gorgeous girl regularly visits me, and she's the only one to date who achieves full and complete satisfaction while seated in the apparatus. Her case is unique – it alone is my reward for so many disappointments. Our young friend today is fascinating, but she is still fantasizing about possession. For me that detracts greatly from the interest. For you, perhaps … I'm going to get my collection ready …"

He hesitated before departing.

"I'll leave you for a moment. If you like …"

At that he went out of the room, his sentence unfinished. Margo came up to me but the other man motioned to her.

"Leave us, please."

She looked worriedly at me. I made a sign to her to leave. When we were alone, the man leaned over to me.

"Raise your legs in the air."

I obeyed him. He ordered me to assume ever more acrobatic postures and when he considered that I was sufficiently at his mercy he made me keep still. Then, bearing down on me, he began to kiss the part of me I was already offering him at the expense of acute discomfort. His tongue did not need to scour me for long. My head seemed to explode. I fantasized that the man licking me so methodically was Marc, which considerably increased my excitement. I groaned with pleasure and he waited until I was almost coming before he penetrated me violently.

Each of his thrusts drove me back so that my head slammed against the metal frames of the chair. I bit my lip in the effort not to cry out, while he went faster and faster. I opened my mouth wide to scream with pleasure but at that very moment he sank deeply into me and stopped moving. From the pulsations of his prick I sensed that he was ejaculating inside me and I succeeded in catching him up at the peak of his pleasure, I too melting in an extraordinary orgasm. The man withdrew brutally, wiped his prick against my belly, readjusted his clothing and left the room without addressing a word to me.

A loud humming was audible and the picture on the large screen reappeared. The video film replayed in slow motion the scene I had just lived. The man pulled out his stiff prick and entered me so slowly that I bit my lip. Then followed the deliberate, powerful movements of that demonic possession. I observed them all, fingering myself voluptuously in search of a new climax. I managed to synchronize the timing of my second orgasm and lost consciousness just when the hugely enlarged organ spurted its milky tides deep within my reddened flesh.

CHAPTER FIVE

I stayed home for a very long time after that incident, not going out at all. I washed myself in a purifying bath. I prayed to the Virgin, begging for absolution. I repented. I could have died of shame and desperation. I wanted to cancel the power of speech, to become blind so that I could remain in the dark and forget what I looked like. I wanted to be empty once again, so as to rediscover the taste and texture of childhood strawberry jams, of mother's pullover, of delicious homemade soup – of everything that reassures, warms and banishes fear.

A terrible conviction overwhelmed me: I was certain I had somehow irrevocably turned a page of my life. It was the end of an era. I would no longer behave as I had done for years. My shame and disgust became unbearable after Margo sent me the four 500 franc notes which paid me for my pleasure and humiliation. I swore I would surrender, I'd give everything I had to succeed. I wanted to win Marc over. For him I would renounce my freedom, offer as sacrifice my solitude, patience and abstinence. I wouldn't chase men any longer. I wouldn't give way to the pleasures I adored. I wanted to be renewed, innocent, frustrated, available. In love.

I grew pale and lost weight. Those who had featured in my superficial life began to avoid me. I was no longer funny or available. Whenever the phone rang I would pick up the receiver and remain silent.

"Hello. Joy?"

" – "

"Hello, is that you Joy? Answer me!"

" – "

"Come on Joy, answer, I know you're there. What's happening anyway? Don't you recognize me?"

The monologue would turn into a drama. When it became absurd or tiresome I would hang up without having uttered a single word. I went through a tidying up phase. I rearranged my photograph albums, carefully classifying by year all the negatives of the men I'd been involved with. I reread old letters, burning all the lies. Whenever it grew dark I would dream about catching flu, with runny eyes, blocked-up nose and all, so that mother might return as in the old days, bringing me vegetable broth or rum-laced milk, and stay beside me until I went to sleep. I would have liked to indulge my every whim without anyone objecting. I used to imagine that one day Marc would grace my tiny hideaway, declaring:

"I knew you were ill and I've come to look after you!"

But I remained alone like an elderly spinster, my hair in need of a wash under my tatty headscarf.

One day Margo interrupted my retreat.

"What's happened to you? You're deathly pale and you must have lost about three stone! My God, you're ill!"

I pushed her towards the bed, looking beadily at her. She was sun-tanned and glowing with rude health.

"I've just got back from Los Angeles. It was great."

"What about David?" I asked her mildly.

"Torture, my love. He gets more and more stupid, vain and neurotic every day. Absolute hell! Stop me if I'm going on about him too much, it's hard for me not to. How about you?"

For the first time for ages I let myself go. As I carried on griping about my misfortunes I saw her big eyes goggle and her jaw drop. Then she recoiled.

"But ... are you in love? Oh no," she exclaimed disgustedly, "not that, not *you*!"

" Yes. Me," I replied mournfully.

"But Joy, you haven't thought it over properly, it's *dangerous*. And it's just not done. In love! Girls like us get taken for a ride if we let ourselves fall in love. We just have to look good and smile well, and we simply must keep stable and healthy ... but really Joy, falling in love, what crass stupidity!

43

Do you *realize* what it means? When you love someone you can't be self-centred any more, you have to think of the other person and what might give them pleasure. And it messes things up so much: you can't take off on trips, or go out any more in the evenings, you quarrel with everybody ... And don't imagine you'll get any thanks for it from your lover. He takes everything as his right. He'll become more and more demanding, sometimes he'll get jealous, you realize. Anyhow, he'll no longer make an effort, he'll get dozy, and then, Joy my love, you'll have *the* most appalling drama on your hands! *He's* gained the upper hand. It's a losing battle and one day you cease to please and no longer want to."

Margo came over to pet me. Her eyes shone moistly.

"You know what happens then, Joy? You find yourself alone again, abandoned. Old. No man is worth all that – no man girls like us meet, anyhow. The sort of love you're thinking of is for others, girls who work an eight-hour day and go home by Métro, tired out and nerve-wracked. They come home just when *we're* going out; they cook their meal just when we're putting the final touches to our make-up, and they go to sleep when we're coming alive. Forget it Joy, clear out, take off quick, because you're in danger. Make yourself scarce before he eats you up – only to turn you into good faithful little wifey, the deceived drudge. Tell me you're not about to start loving one man exclusively when we can have them all – are you, Joy my love?"

I began laughing. Margo stared at me absolutely aghast.

"*You* can't understand, Margo. You'll never fall in love, you go around picking everything to pieces and you miss out on what's important. If you only knew how good it feels to love a guy! So that each morning before you even open your eyes, he's there on your mind. Now I have an aim in life. A long struggle may be in the offing, but believe me I won't do him any favours. I want him to myself, for myself alone, and I'll have him. I'm beginning to understand war, crime, and death. Loving is a bit like all three at once. And so much the better if he doesn't deserve it: my victory will be all the greater. I only wish one thing: that one day you'll feel the

44

same way."

"It's awful," Margo said. "If you really mean what you say, you've got to pull yourself together!"

"No, it's too late now."

Margo departed, much as one leaves somebody terminally ill. She seemed sad yet falsely bright, as if to say: "You'll need all your courage, but you can always count on me." I already knew, however, that I could no longer rely on anybody but myself.

Next day I wrote mother a long letter, which I don't often do, because she never answers. But I wanted her to know about Marc. While writing to her it occurred to me that I knew nothing about him, not even his name, so I had to invent a bit. I'm rather good at that, though.

To sublimate my solitude I had the urge to see fine things: I visited the Louvre, the Musée de l'Homme, Victor Hugo's house and the Musée Carnavalet. I spent hours in front of gloomy pictures. I listened to classical music, read books which left their mark on me and which I've never dared open since. I wrote three poems and recited them to myself in front of a mirror. Sometimes I would weep uncontrollably. At night I'd fall asleep talking to him: "I see you lying in bed, darling. You're tired and sad, you smoke a cigarette which you stub out in the ashtray and that movement of yours makes the sheet slip off your body. When you switch off the light you'll see in your dreams that full-breasted girl you didn't stay with. My darling that was me, and till the end of my life I'll be close to you to kill you with love and pleasure."

August ended slowly in the dusty heat of the big city. I often thought about our huge deserted house with its shutters closed. I saw once again those holidays of my childhood – the evenings ended in mornings in an unfamiliar room. I remembered returning to Paris: getting up at dawn, the last sight of the clump of trees obscuring the house, and the sickly

45

flavour of the sweets I used to suck throughout the long journey back. Mother would drive, chainsmoking, and continually asking: "Joy my love, you're not too sad are you?"

The morning the Parisian summer holiday ended I noticed increased traffic in the streets. Children were tanned and mothers had gained weight. The baker on the corner had rolled up the iron shutter of his shop window. In my letter box I found a postcard from mother and a miraculous cheque from an advertising agency for which I'd done some photos before the vacation.

That whole day I played at being rich. I took taxis and bought myself flowers. In the evening Alain called round. He too had returned from his holidays and his first visit was to me. Alain is my best male friend, my big brother, accomplice and confidant. He understands me before I even need to speak, makes me laugh when I'm sad and knows the right moment to take his tactful leave if I'm happy. We've lived next door to each other for ages, and while I'd give him a lung if he needed a transplant I think he might even offer me his life. He hugged me, laughing.

"You've grown even taller. You've become quite hot stuff!"

I snuggled into his reassuring shoulder and talked to him for hours about Marc. He listened to me, smiling to start with, more seriously as time wore on. He said nothing, but looked at me hard and long before leaving. I realized he was upset. This troubled me and I had difficulty getting to sleep. I caressed myself, thinking of Marc. When I awoke the next day it was September.

I received a letter from Marc. Agog with curiosity, I examined the envelope for a while before opening it, since I didn't recognize the handwriting. One white sheet of paper had been folded into four, and in the centre tiny little blue lettering began dancing in front of my eyes. He had written:

46

Woman listen to your heart. Read no other book. And below this the magic words: *I'm thinking of you, Marc.* He had clumsily drawn in a small heart.

I was quite won over, of course. I felt stunned, wildly happy, as I studied the envelope for a finger-print. I pored over the postmark – 19.30 the previous evening, Rue Balzac. I went into raptures on seeing my own name written out by him for the first time: Mlle Joy Laurey. Was this note his first sign of weakness? Was it the white flag waving from his citadel? Would the enemy surrender? Some hope!

It was the evening of Alain's birthday. I'd bought him a gold Dunhill key-ring, squandering the rest of my money on this present. When he opened the packet I saw that he was really delighted: he looked quite moved, and took my hand.

"I'll keep your – our – housekeys on it."

What he'd said amazed me. He took advantage of that to embrace me. I frowned, as if I hadn't understood, but he held me tight and whirled me round and round off my feet, like something out of that film *A Man and A Woman*. He nuzzled my neck – and he smelt nice, of lavender – so I felt at ease. Then he launched off on a long speech:

"Joy you really must change your life-style ..."

I didn't listen because I was fascinated by his lips as they shaped words and moved up and down over his dazzling teeth in rhythm to the words. I fantasized that it was Marc's mouth and lips, Marc talking:

"Joy, you need a man who's as strong as a rock, who'll understand you and help you grow. You're still so frail, Joy my love. Your house will have a huge chimney and it'll be surrounded by flowers and have a bed so large that you'll have to search hard to find him ..."

"Find whom?" I asked, suddenly interested.

"Your rock. Your man."

I tried to be kind.

"I'd like him to have eyes like yours. I like your eyes ..."

My God, what had I just said!

"You're all the same," he retorted bitterly, continuing:

"As soon as a man gets fond of you, he doesn't interest you

47

any more. What you need is indifference, coolness. Keeping aloof and inaccessible is the way to get you. Life's fucked up if it means cheating, lying, and messing about. Shit!"

He left without another word or a backward glance. I wondered why I didn't want to live with him. I'm sure he would have loved me deeply and generously. I shut my eyes, trying to imagine him making love to me, but it was Marc I kept seeing. I was drained, demoralized. I missed this invisible man.

I walked – went walking everywhere, climbing stairs, crossing avenues, waiting for green lights to turn red. I sat in squares full of children and meditated in empty churches. I went onward like a pilgrim, unconcerned about tiredness or heat, and firm in my faith. I placed one foot in front of the other, knowing I was going somewhere but not knowing where.

I sat on the terrace of a brasserie and ordered bread and water. I was turning into a mystic. After avidly consuming a *croque monsieur* and a coca cola, I picked up a magazine left behind on a chair – and opened it at a glossy, full page colour photo of myself. That gorgeous scantily clad young woman was myself: my bottom jutted provocatively, my bare back was oiled and sleek, and I looked free and arrogant. I stared at myself admiringly, screwing up my myopic eyes then, as I glanced up, I caught sight of him.

My heart turned over and my head reeled. I flung some change into my neighbour's glass, stubbed out my cigarette in the mustard, and trampled on scores of luckless feet before reaching the pavement. I started running. Out of breath, I shouted hoarsely:

"Marc, Marc, please wait!"

He turned round, then stopped. My momentum carried me on and I crashed straight into his arms: I wouldn't have minded dying there and then. Nothing would ever be more beautiful than the moment I had just lived through.

We walked together hand in hand, silent and apprehensive, waiting for some irreversible and definitive words to capture the moment. The day had turned grey; it was dusk when we found ourselves sitting on a bench facing the Seine. We were utterly alone together. A barge's hooter boomed over the sparkling water.

"Marc, I don't want to leave you ever again. I'll follow you everywhere, go where you like, but I don't want us to be parted. I need to see you and hear your voice. Answer me Marc," I begged him tremulously.

I had just made that declaration I'd laboriously been preparing all through my adolescence, in the privacy of that brass-bedded room under the slate roof of our house in the Dordogne. In my girlish dreams this fine speech was addressed to a godlike sun-bronzed figure handsomer than an ancient Greek statue, with skin softer than velvet – and now I was confronting a man like any other, neither tall nor handsome nor a god. Yet he was the one I loved and at that moment I knew that the gods of Olympus themselves couldn't have stirred me more.

He had a dismal little flat in a bourgeois block situated in the dull Plaine Monçeau *quartier*. The varnished double doors opened on to a hall, leading to a sitting-room which in turn gave on to the bedroom adjoining the bathroom. There was furniture everywhere, numerous chairs and armchairs, records stacked against one wall, green indoor plants and red curtains, a sofa. I ought to have noticed some disturbing details – the page of the magazine open at my photo, lying on the telephone table, and my phone number scrawled across a notebook. I ought to have waited for his answers to the questions I had asked him. I should have insisted that he break the melodramatic silence. I should have lied, played around a bit, flirted. I should even have left. Should have, could have.

I set upon him industriously, undressing him as if he were a small boy. His body was warm, smooth and soft, with a faint aroma of cachou. My mouth embarked upon a long journey while I was rubbing my palms over his shoulders, across his chest and along his buttocks. His torso was as beautiful as in a stylized Crucifixion: he was awaiting death. I was becoming familiar with his skin, and I watched out for his reactions and

49

responses, testing his sensitivity. I traversed this *terra incognita* with the agonizing pleasure an explorer must feel when crossing uncharted desert for the first time.

I took his prick between my hands and rubbed it, moistening it with my tongue and even venturing to kiss it. Marc closed his eyes. I placed the stiffening sex against my forehead and stared at it greedily, murmuring crazy things to it I'd never thought of before and which I'll never be bold enough to write down. I positioned it in my mouth and with one long splendid slide it drove towards the back of my throat. Then it plunged further still, seeming larger than ever. I feared it would choke me, my eyes filled with tears but those tears no longer had anything to do with love: I was about to die, that prodigious thing in my mouth was beating like a heart. I bore down tightly upon that rigid flesh which I worshipped like a pagan – prey for the first time to that obsession which has plagued me ever since. I like imagining the mystic separation of the male from his sex, so that I kiss, suck, eat *only* that piece of flesh distinct and separate from a body; I enjoy destroying the erection, swallowing the prick, devouring the red and threatening member I adore. The object makes me experience a basic need, that of giving my mouth until it fills with the semen whose creamy blandness can drive me wild.

Marc sighed deeply. I speeded up my rhythm, bobbing to and fro, sucking him as hard as I could, then I would stop abruptly and rub my lips unbearably slowly along the entire length of his shaft. Marc tensed, burying his fingers in my hair, and groaned: "Joy, I'm coming."

He appeared to collapse, seeming suddenly fragile and vulnerable as he flooded my mouth and his sperm ran down my face, dripping on to my breasts. He twisted his body to break away from me, but I did not want to let him go and I continued to drink, suck and inhale him, as if drawing sustenance from that warm seed which issued from the very depths of his being. I was smeared with his sweet effusion; I licked his body, and rubbed against him with my sopping wet sex like an animal, a bitch adoring her mate. He propped himself on one elbow, pushed me back, opened me up and thrust himself deep into my vagina. It hurt. He said:

"Look at me. Open your eyes. Look."

I saw his face as he leaned over me – it was indistinct, vaguely uneasy, and his pupils seemed dilated. He penetrated me slowly: with each movement I uttered a cry which became more and more urgent and highpitched as I approached my moment of truth. We were taking stock of one another: our same hatred, our same ugliness. I felt myself on the very brink, sensing that nothing could now delay that explosion which would annihilate me. Had I been on the verge of death I'd have come first, come what may – and I bit him fiercely, scratching him with my nails in the fury of my paroxysm. He reared above me, becoming gigantic, and then a wave seized hold of me, I was totally unable to control myself any longer and, devastated, I fainted away.

Long afterwards, as I regained consciousness, I also seemed to gain insight. I intuitively knew that my life so far had been nothing but a series of clumsy mistakes and disillusion.

Marc brushed my lips with his.

"You're a strange girl!"

"I don't know what happened then. I've never felt anything like that before. I've never reacted quite like that – it was so different. So different from other times, from the others."

He smiled, holding me close. I breathed in his male smells, thinking: he mustn't move, everything must begin again, as at the movies when THE END appears on screen and everyone knows the programme will recommence, and seeing the film once more I'll cry all over again just like before. It's crazy how easily I can cry at the movies.

Marc rose and drank about a bottleful of water. He winked at me and shut himself in the bathroom. I listened to the horrible racket all showers seem to make whenever men use them. I rushed after him, knelt down and began drying him, using a sheet as towel.

"Joy, I'm going to leave Paris. I'm off to New York next

week. Or at the end of the month. I'll write."

I froze like an idiot, with my hands out in front of me.

"Have you had a look at the weather? It'll rain, for sure. What a drag, eh? What's the matter Joy?"

He frowned as he was getting dressed.

"When I saw your photo in the magazine – the one where you're modelling underwear – it had a strange effect on me. I wanted to see you again."

He smiled and buttoned his shirt.

"My best friend, Didier, didn't believe that we ... you and I, that is ... that we really knew each other. I told him that one day we'd all have dinner together. Would you like that?"

My sigh was supposed to warn him.

"Cut it out!"

"What? What's the matter?"

"Forget it. I just don't want to listen to you any more. I'm leaving."

I seldom lose my temper. I tend instead to brood or complain but when I *am* angry the results can be spectacular.

"You're crazy. What did I say?"

"A load of crap. Nothing of interest. It's unbelievable how stupid men become when they've just got laid."

"Stop talking like that. If you want to go, go: I won't stop you."

I dressed in a rush, my jeans impeding me, my sweater inside out.

"That does it, I'm going. It's better this way. Goodbye for good. How could I have imagined I loved you? I must be mad!"

White with rage he followed me to the door, his arms dangling by his sides, with all the charm of the male about to move in for the kill.

"Mad, yes, no doubt about that. But a whore too. Did you want me to believe you were in love? You must be joking!"

I turned round furiously as I was opening the door.

"What do you know about love, or about women?"

"Not a lot, maybe, but I know how to distinguish between a normal woman and a slut."

Disgusted by his vulgarity I turned my back on him and went down the stairs. He leaned over the bannister and without raising his voice delivered the parting shot:

"I saw those photos you agreed to do for your own kicks. A tart would have turned the job down. You know what you can do with your love!"

He slammed the door. I staggered against the stair-rail, my forehead pressing against it, feeling utterly shaken. I recalled those poses I'd had to adopt during that evening. I remembered just how clear, how detailed, each shot was, and despite myself I felt excited once more because I knew that Marc too had been excited and that it was probably thanks to the photos that he'd wanted to see me again. The door opened and Marc, eyes blazing with anger, leaned over to throw down my handbag.

"Here, you forgot something."

"Marc," I managed to whisper.

"What now?"

"It's true, you know. I love you."

He paused, then came slowly downstairs towards me. Grasping me by the shoulders he stared fixedly into my tear-filled eyes.

"Come on. Forgive me. I didn't mean to say that to you."

"But that's what you were thinking. It doesn't matter, anyhow."

He more or less held me up until I reached the settee, made me sit down on it very carefully, like an old woman, and then fell by my knees.

"Joy, I like you, I've never desired a woman so much ..."

"*I* love you."

He sighed heartrendingly and rubbed his head against my knees.

"I love you too, but what's the use, you have your life and I have mine. What could we do together, other than make love? I never know what hour I might return, I travel a lot, I have late conferences and meetings. I can't impose all that upon any woman. Naturally when I see you I want to drop everything, grab hold of you and take you off to some desert

53

island. Yet I know I wouldn't stay there long. I like my work, I like my life. Above all I like my independence. I can't imagine a woman following me everywhere, being behind every door I opened, or in every bed I slept in. You and I as a couple, Joy – it's impossible."

I replied that I was in no hurry, that anyhow I'd be the stronger, and that I was ready to give up everything. Which would be easy since I had very little: I could follow him and wait for him.

"I like my way of life, too," I continued. "And my freedom. But if you're there I don't give a damn about freedom because my freedom is you. Do you understand?"

He took me in his arms and hugged me very tightly. He caressed my hips and buttocks, sighing:

"I should have warned you ..."

He kissed me again, then he pulled down my jeans and leaned me back on the settee. I felt his prick urgent between my thighs. Once more I bit my lip so as not to cry out.

"When I saw those photos," he remarked in a strained, rather hoarse voice, "I thought I'd go crazy. I wanted you so much ... Would you do the same things for me?"

I shut my eyes, not fighting whatever fate had in store. So I said something loudly to him which I never usually say because somehow it always sounds vulgar to me: "Fuck me Marc!"

CHAPTER SIX

One Monday morning at eight, Marc left for New York. I accompanied him to Roissy, feeeling shivery and full of cold, my nose red and eyes streaming. I clung to his arm and kept asking him quietly: "You'll come back soon, won't you? Will you write to me?"

He answered "Yes, of course, of course," as he searched for his passport and embarkation card. I'd promised him I wouldn't go out, I'd be faithful to him and I'd think of him every night before going to sleep.

"What about you," I said to him, "you'll think of me, won't you, over there?"

He kept reassuring me that yes, of course he would. I'd clasp his hand very hard and he'd gently disengage it, winking playfully at me. I dashed off to buy him magazines – *Playboy*, *Penthouse* and *Lui* – drawing his attention to one of them. "Look, that's me." He took the magazine and glanced at it, shaking his head:

"You're really the most beautiful one there. It's true, Joy, it's you I like best ..."

That made me happy. Groups of travellers with their hand luggage were waiting by the embarkation gates, all managing to look glum and sleepy. I told myself that I'd never be sad if I could only leave with him. I'd have loved to surprise him by saying: "Hey, I've bought a ticket and I'm coming with you."

I didn't have the money, of course, nor would I have dared to be so presumptuous. I asked him if he knew any girls in New York, and he replied:

"I'm going there on business, you know, and I really don't have time for all that."

Then, after a pause, he added:

"In any case, I don't need any other girls."

I knew very well that he was lying, but it pleased me all the same. We sat down and he made me promise to work hard.

"If you stir yourself a bit – what with your style and figure – you could really make it to the top. Wouldn't you like to be the most famous model of them all?"

I shook my head, because I had a bad cold and I don't enjoy being photographed. It means long hours and it's depressing work. I'd like to be something other than a top model, I didn't fancy just earning a crust till I was forty only to be told one day that I was too old.

"I promise you I'll make a big effort," I lied. Then I added: "You'll see I'm serious: one day maybe I'll be able to work with *you*!"

He looked up at the sky, hearing that.

"Business is no joke," he said. "You'd soon get bored if you involved yourself in business matters every day ..."

True. I have forgotten to properly introduce Marc Charroux. He's in business. He told me that his work consists of fund-raising for industrialists, producers, artists – for people who already have quite enough money, in fact. So he deals in factories as often as toothpaste, films or ski-lifts. I'd have liked to see him at work. I felt I could have become his assistant. I imagined myself wearing huge black-framed glasses, repelling persistent female visitors who had waited hours for an appointment:

"No, it's not possible. Monsieur Charroux regrets he is snowed under at present. I'm sorry, but *we* have to catch the plane for Bogotá in an hour."

I pictured myself showing him his appointments diary and telling him we had an hour to kill, whereupon he'd make love to me on his executive couch before calling the huge black limousine driven by a brooding, silent chauffeur.

Concorde was late, so we went to the bar for a drink. I wanted to lay my head on Marc's knees. A man approached, however, exclaiming: "Charroux, no, it can't be!"

They walked off to the other side of the room where they

remained deep in discussion for the best part of an hour. Then Marc beckoned me over to rejoin them. He introduced me: "Chief, let me introduce Joy Laurey, the model."

He went on rather heavily and the Chief, who looked as though he'd earned the title, nodded with evident and considerable elation.

"Yes, indeed, so I see."

I stifled all my fine words of farewell while Marc kissed me on the forehead, cursorily and absently, muttering "Bye, see you soon," and disappeared with the appalling Chief. I hated that interloper as I stood there blowing my nose. I was all alone in the cold hall, dismal as the rain. I was useless, that was the word for it, useless and unimportant.

I realized I hadn't enough money for a taxi so I queued up for an airport coach. I waited an eternity, feeling tired, chilly and ill. I'd broken out into a cold sweat and my heart was thumping. I prayed Marc wouldn't have an accident. I sat beside an overweight Japanese who gave me fitful little nods every so often: hello, hello. I pressed my forehead against the smeared window and watched the autoroute unravel in the rain. Rain and traffic jams – all are meaningless when the man in one's life is flying off to New York.

For a week I double-checked my letter box and stayed within range of the phone. Whenever I did have to leave the flat – just long enough to buy a loaf or some ham slices – I would take the phone off the hook in case Marc rang, so that he could hear the engaged tone and therefore not assume that I wasn't in. I did not, of course, receive a letter, a telegram or a phone call. After a week I gave up and paid Alain a visit. His secretary showed me into his office.

"Would you mind waiting. M. Guichard will be with you presently."

Knowing Alain, I was sure he had begun (and ended) an affair with this young woman who eyed me so aggressively. As soon as she left me on my own I rang the New York hotel where Marc was staying. I had to repeat and spell out his name no less than three times. After a series of unbearable little clicks the receptionist's nasal voice delivered its verdict:

"Mooseyer Sharoo nay ploo ici."

I asked this cretin who spoke French so fluently whether Mooseyer Sharoo had left a forwarding address, but the lout had already rung off.

I sulked somewhat after that, so to cheer me up Alain invited me to a classy restaurant near his place. Foie gras, duck, some fine Bordeaux and armagnac: the chef of the Comte de Gascogne had excelled himself. I got very drunk and my flat little stomach felt like bursting beneath my too-tight dress. I stopped drinking but Alain didn't press me or complain: he smiled and took my hand. As for me, my heart wasn't really in it, though I felt happier. I told him:

"Alain, I get on all right with you."

"Me too."

"Fine."

"I feel the same way, Joy dear."

The cold outside was arctic and I flung my arms around his neck.

"Tonight, friend, I don't want to go back to my place."

"Where do you want to go?"

"To yours."

He placed me in his car like a precious and unwieldy parcel and we drove off, windscreen-wipers ticking, radio blaring.

He stopped in front of a rusty gate.

"This is my new home."

Alain waved proudly at the tall villa, built in that stonework dear to the Parisian suburbs. With its steeply sloping pointed roof, it looked like a cross between something from the Middle Ages and a house out of a Hitchcock movie. He opened its front door and carried me through it in his arms.

"Just like a young bride," he whispered, kissing my neck, "crossing the threshold of her house."

I chuckled. He switched on three lamps and I was steeped in a vanilla- and cinnamon-scented cosy warmth. I've always had a keen sense of smell ... He brought me a glass full of bubbly and showed me a remarkable and disturbing painting.

"I bought it because *she* resembles you."

I stared wide-eyed at a huge nude in a baleful pose, her

bosom thrust forward, and with a heart, a sun and various keys emerging from her womb.

"You see," he said, "she's as bizarre as you are. After all, the beautiful is always bizarre."

I was swaying suddenly, and I felt unhealthily drowsy. Alain said:

"Now you ought to sleep."

I agreed, and taking me gently in his arms he carried me upstairs to the bedroom. He laid me on the bed and turned on a soft orange light. There were dried flowers in a glass jar, and gilt knick-knacks with tiny snowstorms of yellowish dust. A musical box tinkled its metallic piano tune, a long way off. While Alain went back down the spiral staircase, I undressed and slid between sheets redolent of violets. I did not hear him come up again, for I was floating on a mauve cottonwool cloud, a rain of moist flowers cascading over me while brown dogs and miniature horses galloped to meet me and lick my palms, their rough tongues tickling me irresistibly. The sun blazing from the organdie ceiling was extinguished. A storm was building up and the fresh breeze hardened my nipples.

"War you doing?" I groaned thickly. "I want smoke some. More. Alll-*ain*, say something!"

The silence scared me. I opened my eyes.

He was lying between my thighs, his tongue tenderly exploring my sex. He was licking me as slowly as those tiny horses had licked my palms, but his tongue was soft, its tip very pointed. The mouth making love to me was opening my vagina, infiltrating within my hot folds, vibrating tentatively. I spread my legs wide, offering myself more generously, and a host of unruly sensations overwhelmed me. Heavy lips were burying themselves between my buttocks, unbearable tickles assailed my downy mount, and the tip of that long tongue burrowed into me while fingers joined the fray, feeling me, stroking, rubbing and finally sinking inside me. I cried out and my long legs kicked helplessly as a tidal wave surged through my loins. The restless mouth alternated between one opening and the other, covering me in warm, sticky saliva, until my orgasm caught me by surprise, sooner than I thought

59

possible, and I writhed and fell forward with my face deep in the violet-scented pillow.

Then Alain slowly rubbed against me and I turned to grasp hold of him. He had anticipated my caress and I bent forward to graze upon his engorged virility, which would have alarmed an innocent adolescent but which only increased the excitement of one who was no more than a misunderstood and much-criticized little whore. I dug my nails into the stiffened flesh to provoke a cry which was not forthcoming, and then I tried to take him in my mouth. He pushed me away, however, saying: "I've loved and wanted you for so long!"

He turned me over, forcing apart my narrower entrance, and inch by inch took possession of that painful passage which was waiting for him alone. It seemed, that incredibly slow and painful advance, to last a lifetime. The acute discomfort was immediately soothed then exceeded by the next sensation. In my delirium I tasted the inflamed friction of our united flesh, the yielding of our tensed muscles, the indecent noises of suction, the slipperiness of our wetted membranes, and those intoxicating spicy odours of earthy sex. I was living out my most secret sexual fantasy, in experiencing the conspicuous disproportion of his aggressive member and my tiny vessel. I gloried in his power and my submission. I felt the injustice of the world. I was the castrating female receiving the pain which I had sought to deal out. I wept with shame and rage. I screamed out obscenities to banish from the darkness those pornographic photos all too clearly defined on glossy paper. Then I forgot everything, because suddenly he had started moving, harder, deeper, and my body responded, breasts hanging forward, arms and elbows seeking purchase. The demonic motions broke down and suddenly there was all the frustration of yes and no, love and hate, life and death. I tried to revive, pinned under the dark mass overpowering me, and muttered feebly: "Come on, harder," and at first he didn't hear me or understand.

"Joy my love."

He hammered away at me for a long time after that, after I

60

had felt myself broken, blotted out, demolished. I gradually regained my senses while he continued lunging into my body with awesome force. I was fully conscious once again, further pleasure having eluded me, but still he toiled away. For the first time that evening, Marc's image returned to plague me, and I tensed in order to expel Alain. The latter misinterpreted my movement and promptly came, inundating me with those juices I no longer wanted to receive.

I tried to wait as long as possible before telling him I wasn't in love with him. He lay beside me, calm and relaxed, and so he should have been, yet he was discreetly keeping his distance too: he knew me well, for I didn't dare criticize him. I listened to the clock ticking and the endless scratch and click of the player arm, its stylus repeatedly snagging from the disc's last track.

He laid his hand on my breast, of course. I looked at him from the corner of my eye.

"Alain, I don't love you."

He turned his head towards me and I thought he was smiling.

"I know."

I sensed some spark go out in him at that, and a barrier loomed between us. He certainly knew I didn't love him, but he did mind my saying so. I felt like adding, "You've given me more pleasure than the others, even more than *he* did, but my heart doesn't love you – it's already promised."

Alain stroked my cheek and I seemed to feel a great black cloud over me.

"I think it'd be better if I left."

He did not reply and I dressed, shivering. I hoped just the same that he'd try to stop me or at least say something, but he lay motionless and let me go on downstairs.

I picked up my handbag and walked all the way home over the slippery pavements, soaked by the drizzle, drunk with pleasure and despair.

Marc did not write. Alain no longer rang. Mother stayed on in Lausanne. There was not a word from Margo. I didn't go out, saw nobody and wallowed in remorse. September passed with the ponderous slowness of a badly directed movie. October with roast chestnuts in the chimney-nook was definitely not for me.

I rang Marc at home and heard his voice answer: "Hello. Yes?"

I hung up in panic. I thought: "Go to hell, you swine, you've got back and never even let me know, not a word. I might have died, for all you care."

I was booked for three fashion spreads in quick succession. I met some new girls, tight-arsed mealy-mouthed snobs the lot of them, and was chatted up by the three respective photographers and their five assistants – the sixth being obviously immune to female charms. If they asked questions, I wouldn't reply except when I had to, and then only curtly and reluctantly. They talked to me about my career and my future plans. I told them I really didn't give a fuck – and that shocked them.

One evening at the end of a session a man came up to me. I was nervous, shaking with exhaustion, and my back and arms ached from two hours of stupidly exaggerated poses.

"Name's Mocoroni," he said, "and I've seen you in the magazines. I'm setting up a film with Alexander Goraguine. I might have something to interest you. Would you have dinner with me one evening at the Elysée-Matignon?"

I know only too well why I accepted: I wanted to be in a film, to see my name headlined in all the papers, and above all for Marc Charroux to get a sickening bellyful. The night of the dinner I spent three hours perfecting my make-up and arrived at the Elysée-Matignon on Mocoroni's arm, looking like a Hollywood star, my mouth glossy, my eyes big as butterflies and fluttering too.

Alexander Goraguine couldn't have been smaller if he tried, five foot perhaps, on tiptoe. He was rotund, bald, and his abnormally long arms ended in wiry, clawlike, spell-binding hands: the eye was drawn to and riveted by these, and you grew dizzy following their movements. When he caught sight of us, he rushed forward.

"You're divine! Your eyes are wonderful, my dear, huge and lustrous, just right for the big screen. Cheekbones – turn that way – yes, a wee bit prominent, the light'll catch them, excellent. Your waist is exquisite, breasts perfect! You're so right not to wear a bra. Let's see your legs. Admirable. Long, a little on the thin side perhaps, but that's always popular, the coltish teenager look. Really splendid."

He asked me to sit down. I was exhausted. He ordered a bottle of Dom Pérignon.

"You have star quality, Joy. If you want –"

The meaningful pause was slightly too long.

" – you could build an international career. You're just the type we're looking for right now. The perverse yet well-bred adolescent."

Goraguine burst into laughter. Mocoroni sniggered. I gazed glumly at them. I was bored and I didn't want to build an international career. I wasn't a perverse or well-bred adolescent. I asked nothing of anyone. The only thing in the world I wanted was Marc Charroux. And I didn't have him.

CHAPTER SEVEN

I became a trendy face. I featured in the tabloids as well as the classier weeklies and monthly mags. I appeared on hoardings everywhere, pasted across the huge posters on every other wall of every other big city: I must have grown at least five yards tall. I was interviewed by neurotic women who smoked too much. I was invited to do a Sunday TV chat show guest spot, where I was asked particularly feeble questions. A new biography was created for me: I discovered I had a whole new background of childhood reminiscences, adventures, setbacks and so on, not to mention a serious illness. Photographers went to ingenious lengths to catch a friend kissing me, or a flash of bare breast or exposed thigh. Several film directors invited me for weekends in their Normandy mansions crammed with boring freeloaders. An airline offered me unlimited free travel in exchange for a big set of ads posing in an Airbus. A celebrated designer let me run an account at his fashion house in return for promoting his new line, *Boutique*. A car manufacturer magnanimously lent me one of his luxury fleet provided I drove it myself – but I can't drive. I was also invited to a variety of events at places like Deauville and Monaco. A well-known soap firm was ready to pay me lavishly for modelling nude, covered in its very own lather. I was to be seen at the most exclusive soirées, escorted by smug and stupid men. My lunch dates were booked up a fortnight in advance. Every morning I received presents and invitations. People I didn't know tried to lend me money on the pretext of involving me in fabulous business schemes. A record company pestered me to record a disco version of a classical theme. A local radio station asked me to host an afternoon programme. Producers sent me scripts which never saw the light of day. Rich men offered me money to accompany them to the Bahamas. A famous Lesbian offered me a solid gold chain if I'd promise her a night of love. The shy, the megalomaniac and the sexually peculiar wrote me passionate letters. The curious kept watch outside my flat. I was compared to Greta Garbo, Marilyn Monroe, Twiggy and Farah Fawcett. A cabaret-bar approached me to sound me out about setting up my own one-woman erotic revue. I was also asked to lend my name to a restaurant, a nightclub, a sex-shop, a brand of make-up and a singles bar. A famous singer revealed in a gossip column that he had spent an unforgettable night with me. An old man committed suicide because he could no longer live without my love. I was followed, hounded, criticized, insulted. For six months I lived through a nightmare. At night I would wake up in a cold sweat, terrified that someone was breaking in. Margo 'told all' about our friendship ... Mother, finally, was proud of her little girl. She cut out photos and articles about me and would ring regularly from Lausanne, where she was now living permanently with Albert. I remained on my own, completely alone and distrustful of everyone. I no longer answered the phone and often had bouts of weeping. Six months.

The film I made with Goraguine, in which I had a minor role, was a failure. The suggested projects using my name all came to nothing, one after another. People stopped sending me letters and gifts. The airline company and the designer closed my accounts. Trips were cancelled. Mocoroni, who had represented me during those six hellish months, wrote me a long epistle 'freeing' me from our agreement – when I'd always regarded myself as free in the first place. I was still on my own, but I did pluck up enough courage to see old friends again. They would pat my hand and say: "Don't worry, you're just going through a bad patch."

I moved into mother's six-room flat on the Avenue de Breteuil, a marvellous place, and rent-free. On the financial side, I more or less broke even each month, and was gradually wiping out the debts accumulated during those six crazy months.

Marc re-surfaced on two occasions. He wrote me a letter

congratulating me on my success, which ended:

"I suspect that your activities probably don't leave you any time to see old friends. That's why I'm not suggesting dinner or a weekend. I hate refusals. But I often think about you, Joy. Kisses, Marc Charroux."

I dashed to shout down the phone that he was mistaken, I was waiting for him alone, and that *he* had abandoned *me*.

"Caller, the number you require has been discontinued. Please refer to Directory or Directory Enquiries. Caller, the number ..."

The telephone too was against me. I began writing as though I were giving birth. I spat out my love through the small nib of my fountain pen scratching across the paper. I emptied cartridges full of blue inked love. I covered pages with errors, alterations, deletions, insertions, crossings-out. I italicized, underlined, apostrophized, blurted capital letters as in a fever. I told him I loved him, and my cry for help was more confession than letter, yet I persevered, signed it, folded the paper, licked the envelope and stamp, sniffled over the name, underlined the address. I tucked this Holy Writ, this message in a bottle, into the gaping slot of Post Box 107, *No Newspapers or Printed Matter*.

I waited. I got drunk. In vain. I could have shot myself. I would have preferred my letter to be returned crumpled and grubby, Return to Sender, Gone Away, No Forwarding Address. I never have received back what I've given.

Later I summoned up enough patience to ring Directory Enquiries. The operator appeared to be both deaf and stupid. After a positively millennial pause she announced brightly: "Charroux is listed. I'm not allowed to pass on ex-Directory numbers." Click.

The obligatory itinerary of my decline took in, of course, Le Palace, Les Bains Douches, the Elysée-Matignon, the 78, Le Paradis Latin, and the rest.

One drunken, particularly charming night Goraguine more or less forced me along to the Elysée-Matignon, where the usual cries went up. "Well, if it isn't Joy!" "Look who's here, give us a kiss, darling!" "You're looking as fantastic as ever!"

"Joy my love!"

I passed from hand to hand, mouth to mouth, while the world and his wife groped my arse, tits and thighs. Goraguine showed me off proudly to all and sundry. I knew he used to brag about having laid me, which was quite untrue, although he tried often enough. I'd had to give him the brush-off firmly and unmistakably.

"Alexander, come off it," I'd told him. "Don't spoil our relationship, it's more important than *our* desire."

The way I'd said it, eyes lowered, lips quivering, I was irresistibly sincere. I won out, lucky for me, thanks to the magic word 'relationship', always trumps with a certain kind of pretentious chauvinist ... Anyhow, on this occasion Goraguine sat me down, waving away hovering waiters and hangers-on alike, and handed me the menu. I prepared to toy with the usual Humble Pie of Silly Little Goose, Lineshooter's Sauce, Bluffer's Delight, Trifler's Trifle, and all the other culinary marvels.

Framed within a bevelled, gilt Venetian mirror, Marc's face appeared amid the crowd. I was paralysed and incredulous. He approached, smiling. I thought how handsome, tall and manly he looked. Then he sat down just behind me. I searched feverishly for my spectacles inside my cluttered handbag. When I put them on I thought I'd pass out: it was certainly him, Marc Charroux, at the table behind us.

Alexander Goraguine slithered across towards me.

"Never wear glasses in public, my dear. Glasses take away the mystery."

I fixed him with a nasty stare and at that moment my heart missed a beat, the plot thickened and the course of history took a new turn.

The maitre d'hôtel, blissfully unaware of his role in my drama, gravely heralded the entry of an amazing creature. Marc leaped to his feet. Her beauty remains imprinted on my memory, for in addition to it she possessed a calm elegance which gave her a dreamlike, graceful quality. She had deep blue almost ultramarine eyes, cascades of coppery-red hair and full sulky lips. Everything about her was perfectly in

67

proportion, right down to her dimpled smile and the malicious twinkle in those superb eyes.

Almost in my ear I heard Marc Charroux declare: "I've been waiting here for you, darling. You look stunning."

They kissed each other dotingly enough to seem out of place in this sort of watering-hole, where sincerity of any kind is despised. Hate welled up inside me: the more I studied her, the more beautiful I thought her. I ran through the adjectives for her – delightful, exquisite, sparkling and so on – while for myself I could only supply unattractive, flashy and over-blown. I left my seat abruptly, sweeping Goraguine and the others from my path, and crossed the room like an automaton until I reached the Ladies, where I wept, biting my knuckles so as to choke back the screams that my heart wanted to vomit out.

After quite some time I re-emerged, revisiting the scene of the crime and looking as attractive as I could. He recognized me just as he was kissing her hand – which, I told myself, would be small and white, unlike my great paws. He seemed utterly dumbfounded: I must admit I've never had such an effect on a man in my whole life. Pale and haggard all of a sudden, he managed a sickly grin and immediately turned his attention elsewhere – towards her.

The necessary diversion was brought about by the unexpected arrival of a loud party consisting of a TV personality, a novelist who specialized in bestselling and angst-ridden sagas, and a woman singer notorious for her temperamental outbursts. The TV guy hugged me, the novelist kissed my hand, and the singer called me darling. Our table at once became the centre of attraction and so the meal proceeded wretchedly. I sensed Marc's glances piercing my back, along with even keener ones from *her*. I felt as queasy as if I'd been at sea.

I managed to intercept the maitre d' and asked him as discreetly as I could to find out the name of the girl sitting behind me. I sank to the expedient of calling him by his surname, Riri, which only regulars used. Desperate remedies, and all that. Riri took her in at a glance and bobbed off into outer darkness to pursue his enquiries. The result of these arrived with the Turbot Nantaise.

"Turbot, Mademoiselle?" and he added under his breath: "Joelle Garnier. *Fashion Journal*. New here."

I thanked him with a meaningful nod and became suddenly interested in the animated conversation going on at my table. The most melodramatic situations bring out my sense of humour, and I found myself joking and wisecracking even while watching that hateful couple.

The grand encounter took place in the cloakroom: the set appropriate to the play, as they say. Marc took it upon himself to smile at me. I exclaimed vivaciously:

"Marc, fancy meeting you! How's life?"

We kissed, with exaggerated and innocent pecks on the cheeks, along with some old soldier-style backslapping. He introduced me.

"Joelle, you obviously know Joy. *Who doesn't, actually?* Joy, this is Joelle Garnier, a *good friend*."

I flashed my nicest smile, despite my dry lips. She smiled pleasantly back, sparkling and fizzy like a thirstquenching drink, her mouth melting to reveal tiny pointed teeth. I shook her hand comprehensively: it was indeed small and white. She confided in an undertone:

"We must have lunch together. I'd like to do something on you for my magazine."

"I'd be delighted," I told her at once, while Marc's smile faded.

I scrawled my phone and address on an invoice I dug out of my bag, and we embraced. She smelt of baby talc. I gave Marc, who was staring frantically at me, a mocking look, and swept out, making my exit with theatrical cool, stranding them where they stood as if I were completely indifferent to the pair of them.

We rounded off the evening at Castel's. There I met Alain. He nodded from a distance, not daring to approach. I ran to him, clung to his neck, and covered his face with kisses, running my fingers through his hair, resting my head on his shoulder and cajoling him: "I don't want to go back to *my* place!"

Shortly after that I was lying in his cashmere and silk bedroom with my legs apart. He was gazing at me adoringly and stroking my bare thighs. He seemed fascinated by my sex which was bathed in an apricot glow from the lamp nearby. I laid my hand flat against his virility, by way of saying sorry.

"My back aches. Would you give me a massage?" I asked him very softly, already imagining his mouth on my vagina. I really needed the pleasure he would bring me. He knelt over me to massage the small of my back and I moulded myself to his hands as they moved over my haunches and then beyond. I felt his fingertips reach my pubic hairs then he speeded up his movements. At the beginning his fingers almost bruised me, but when they moved on to my moist labia, I arched my back still further, and his hand entered me and pleasure overtook us.

Next morning I was woken by the endless ringing of the telephone. I was drowsy and languid because I'd smoked too many of the joints Alain had rolled. I vaguely recalled taking a taxi home after making love twice and feeling considerably better than I had done for months. I'd left Alain sleeping heavily like a satisfied tomcat. The taxidriver had given me a lullaby rendition of *Arrivederci Roma* during the ride back, and I promptly passed out on top of my bed without getting undressed. I picked up the phone with trepidation, shivering a little, because I'd guessed who it was before he spoke.

"I'm coming over," he said, hanging up.

Marc Charroux, Act 3, Scene 3.

I stumbled to the bathroom and slipped under the shower, using gallons of cold water to revive myself.

He rang twice. Two very short rings. I went to the door, reflecting that it was the very first time he had ever rung my doorbell. We gazed at one another through the half-open door like cat and mouse, pursuer and pursued. He pushed me back gently so I'd let him in. He stroked my cheek somewhat furtively, a rather insincere smile on his face. Then he stopped on the threshold of the sitting-room, shaking his head.

"Your mother's place? Comfortable and Swiss."

I was amazed.

"How did you guess?"

70

"A photo of Geneva, one of Lausanne, the poster of Basle ..."

"My stepfather's a redhaired Swiss with a crewcut and bifocals," I informed him. "Would you like something to drink?"

"Coffee, if you've got some."

"I'll make it."

"I'll keep you company."

We drank coffee, sitting on the edge of the sitting-room sofa. He took two sugars and stirred for a long time, his spoon tinkling against the light brown porcelain. My hands were shaking and I needed a cigarette.

"I've been wanting to see you," he declared.

A remarkable thing then happened. Lightheaded as I was, and gripped by a dreadful sense of unease, I seemed to be viewing the scene from a great height – and this ethereal detachment produced the sudden revelation that the man facing me was a stranger. This was no longer the Marc of my nightmare-ridden sleep. I had a flash of intuition, a sharp certainty that my passion was only a form of optical illusion, a shift of perspective. Immediately one looked at it from an angle other than my own, it would lose all significance and become ridiculous, infinitely trivial, banal.

I felt sheer anguish: I'd given too much to be so disillusioned. For a whole year my life had been hanging by a thread and he was that thread. If it happened to break I would collapse irrevocably. I watched him desperately, as if trying to fix in my memory the last moments of someone who is dying. I stared at him so intently that he ceased talking. He grasped my hand. I at once regained confidence: I'd just understood, had got the message conveyed by the contact of that heavy reassuring hand.

My emotional craving did not succeed in precipitating my obsession. I was drawn to him as by a magnet: he represented the only real opponent I had met hitherto. Marc was a sort of final conflict, a last duel. I didn't know how to fight. Nor had everything been said. The gunfight sequence never comes at the start of the western but at the end, when all has been

71

explained and good and bad carefully distinguished and identified. I did not know whether Marc was hero or villain, but now I was convinced that he had a supporting role and was, in Hollywood terms, a guest star. He was only the physical materialization of the myth he represented for me, and as such would be with me for the rest of my life. Nothing could help me escape him.

"I've been wanting to see you," he repeated. "I hadn't forgotten you you know, but something was stopping me coming back to you."

"I know."

The interrupted symphony struck up again even more irresistibly. Violins were playing once more. My heart began beating again and my aberration took hold of me anew. I loved his green eyes even more, his small nose and wilful lips too. The clichés of my love trooped on mechanically – these naïve and garishly coloured commonplaces were overwhelming me, taking over my life. I was on the point of sinking down on one knee and asking him if he would marry me, keep me as servant or slave – anything as long as I was in some way his.

A gesture of his hand stopped me.

"You know, Joy, that I'm in love with another woman. You have to know. I could never lie to you."

In thrillers sometimes the hero is shot in the back and goes on walking while the audience is in suspense, unable to believe that he, the hero, has actually been hit. Then suddenly he collapses and one sees that his back is covered in blood. I turned into a heroine of that sort. I continued talking and asking him questions – where had he met her, was she the girl of the previous evening – but I was the only one to know I'd been hit, my back was bleeding, and I would soon collapse.

"You, I don't want to lose you, though. I'd like it to be as before; I want to love you. I've so much love in my heart *for both of you* ..."

I had enough strength left to smile.

"Yes Marc, yes, but not now, later maybe."

I kissed him, my icy lips on his burning ones. Slowly I showed him to the door, murmuring, "And I love you Marc, I love you too."

I shut the door again and collapsed – shot in the back for sure. He would never turn to me for help or comfort if hurt or ill, whispering "Joy-my-love."

CHAPTER EIGHT

Those who throw away opportunities are never forgiven. I was harshly criticized. The crowd of hangers-on during my headier days of success shunned me like the plague. There was nothing left to see: move on, move on. I was well aware that I'd ruined an important meeting, but I knew that the main reason for this was my inability to adapt. Success is never a matter of luck or the product of a winning streak. I know of no authentic and durable success which is undeserved, nor are there very many unrecognized talents.

Greedy speculators had constructed a precarious scaffolding around me, without worrying about the dangers to myself, the fragile building at the centre of it all. I had nothing going for me but my looks. The rest of me was far more worthwhile, but only of use to myself and for myself. I'm not trained as an actress or singer, I can't dance – and yet they tried to make me a *star*. I am the *anti-star*. I have the employee's mentality, for I don't seek responsibilities or fame, still less do I look for problems. I consent to turn up to a photographer's studio and work there. When the session is over I want to go back home or take a trip out into the country, to sleep or to indulge my fantasies and fancies. Nothing else interests me. The showbiz crowd and the other parasites spent six months trying to understand that. After which I was *out*.

The only person still interested in me after the let-down was Alexander Goraguine. True, he had made a major investment in me and hoped to recoup some of his losses. He proved to be remarkably resourceful during the bad time I went through. He encouraged me firmly, demolished my feeble excuses and arguments, and made me admit that the only way I could get out of the mess I was in was not to ruin everything completely.

"Joy darling, don't let yourself go. A great soldier once said: 'To accept the idea of defeat is to be defeated'."

He persuaded me to leave with him for New York, insisting for so long that I gave in out of sheer exhaustion.

"Joy darling, it's *our* last chance."

Nothing was keeping me in Paris any longer: mother was living in Lausanne, since when I'd only seen her for one weekend. I'd have liked to rejoin her in Switzerland but she never suggested I should and I never asked her. We spoke on the phone for a long time before my departure, and she played her big scene:

"You know Joy, I'm getting on, and I'm worried about not seeing you again. Watch out for the blacks and don't take drugs. Put a little money aside for your return ticket. Must you *really* go, just when everything was working out so well for you in Paris ...?"

"But mother, it's not like it was before. We're apart now anyhow. *You* were the one who left, mother. Anyway, if I'm in Paris or New York, what difference does it make?"

"You won't think I don't love you any more, will you?"

"No, no, it's not that – just that we don't live as we used to, I'm on my own now."

I wound the telephone wire around my finger and couldn't help asking her the burning question which had been on my mind for so many years:

"Do you still remember father?"

We never used to talk about him. I'd never dared broach this taboo subject. Long seconds of silence confirmed her embarrassment.

"Of course I remember your father. He was nice-looking, you know. You take after him. He had a sort of strength – one felt safe with him. I've never felt quite like that with other men ..."

I asked her shyly, gently so as not to annoy her:

"Have you known a lot of men?"

She forced a laugh.

"Oh, Joy! ... men are much of a muchness, you know. They give you almost the same thing, they all want the same proofs, the same sacrifices. What makes them different is us. The same man is different with every woman, but men on their own, individually, are very much alike. I never reckoned them much, hardly looked at them except for your father, but he was the exception. With him it was unique and lasted briefly. Now I'm old and thinking about the future, I've become very attached to Albert. But why this talk of your father?"

"Would you recognize him if you saw him today?"

"Of course I would , Joy."

"And if you did see him again, would you go off with him again?"

"No, Joy, I wouldn't. One must never take a step back. And I think I'd love him too much, still. That is men's great fear – being loved more than they love. Love causes fear in men and women alike, Joy, when it's too extreme."

When mother had hung up, I felt depressed. I stuffed my suitcase full of useless, cumbersome objects and folded my new dresses inside out, a silly superstition with me. I called my friends and said my goodbyes: yes I was definitely leaving and they weren't to forget me, I'd be back some day perhaps ... I went to bed without eating, all alone in the large cold bed. Before I went to sleep I had to ring Alain.

"I'm going. You don't mind, do you?"

"You needed to go."

"Tell me, why must I always spoil the good things? Do you think I'll be happy one day?"

"In time, when you understand that it's pointless to fight what's written."

"What *is* written?"

"That I love you, Joy. I love you with all my strength, body and soul. Whether you're here nor not. I always have."

"And that's written?"

"I promise you that one day you'll love me too."

"But I love you already, Alain. Not with all my heart,

though; not with all of me."

"You come and see me each time you feel bad. You go away again when you're feeling better. One day you'll be incurable and then you'll stay. And I'll be the one to look after you to the end. The end is what matters."

I fell asleep that night dreaming of the skyscrapers of New York, as they appear on postcards.

We flew Concorde. Goraguine sat on my right and clutched my hand convulsively.

"This is a great day, darling. I've just clinched the best deal of my career. We're saved. I'm going to take care of you – right, darling?"

There were caviare canapés, foie gras and toast, glasses of Dom Pérignon. The hostess kept giving me conspiratorial glances. As she leaned across to serve me, her cheek brushed against my hair.

"I have all your photos. I think you're really beautiful ... Are you staying in New York?"

She was attractive, with a soothing voice, and I felt like smiling at her and talking to her but just then Goraguine returned from the toilet, bouncing with childish glee.

"A big contract, Joy. Worth thousands of dollars. You've brought me luck, my darling."

Later on, he confessed.

"I'm in love with you, you know. I can't sleep at night, thinking ..."

I slowly perched my glasses on my nose to assess the damage. Little bald cranium shiny from the strain. Little eyes sparkling with desire, little mouth all moist ... My dark, brooding look must have struck home, for he continued:

"Age and looks aren't obstacles. No Joy, *on the contrary*, take Jackie Kennedy and Onassis ..."

"It killed him," I retorted innocently.

Always superstitious, Goraguine discreetly spat, making the evil eye sign with his right hand.

"Sophia Loren and Carlo Ponti ... I'm ready for anything and everything, if you know what I mean ... to make you forget my age ... and defects ..."

The sledgehammer arguments followed thick and fast:

"I'm a selfmade man, I built everything with my own two hands ... I had nothing to start with, yet no one ever stood in my way, though I was just a poor immigrant. I knew what it was like to go hungry. I bided my time when necessary ... But you're meant for me, Joy!"

I almost yawned, nodding cursorily at what he'd said.

"You startled me, Alexander, I really wasn't expecting all this!"

I pretended to go to sleep. Every so often I watched him through not quite closed eyelids: his eyes never seemed to leave me, and he was fidgeting, moving one hand towards my bare knee and then having second thoughts.

Luckily it was a quick flight and we landed at Kennedy before he'd quite decided to leap on me. A long black limousine awaited us by the exit. It was air-conditioned and had a bar with ice-box and a TV on the blink. The immaculate grey-uniformed chauffeur, his face hidden behind his Ray-Bans, opened and shut the doors for us.

This was the second time I'd set foot upon my adopted country. It crossed my mind that perhaps my father might be driving one of those immense dented vehicles crowding us on all sides of the carriageway.

I discovered the filth of New York, with its streets full of ruts and potholes and those manholes in the middle of the avenues from which jets of steam escaped. Wide-eyed, I came to know all these wonders: the freeway grey with dust which flung itself into the city across a metal bridge; the dirty, deserted streets of Brooklyn; the rude shock of the Manhattan buildings towering overhead. The exquisite sensation of encountering those unknown sights my dreams had made so familiar: Fifth Avenue, Broadway, Times Square, the Empire State Building, Central Park, the Waldorf Astoria. I was fascinated, overwhelmed and stunned. From the start I loved this frightening city as one does one's country. Deep inside, I knew that this discovery was a return.

The limousine took us to the Park Lane Hotel overlooking Central Park. A commissionaire disguised as a coachman hurried to open its doors. I took ages trying to get out of the enormous vehicle and finally I was, in every sense, squirming, for my dress rode up past my thighs and it was quite obvious to one and all that I wasn't wearing knickers! I turned redder than a fire-engine and edged behind Alexander, who was greeting the staff with a regular's nonchalance. After an age the elevator deposited us on the thirty-eighth floor, where I at once observed that the two rooms reserved for us had a connecting door. I smiled malevolently at Alexander and made a dignified entrance into mine.

I suddenly felt homesick, weak at the knees, desperate to run away straight back to Paris. My room was vast, with a bed the size of an aircraft hanger. The windows went on up to the ceiling. Meanwhile behind the half-open connecting door, Alexander's ugly pate shone like a warning light. He was smiling beatifically:

"Joy darling, got everything you need? You must be thirsty! Would you like your dress pressed? A drop of champagne, perhaps? I'll switch on the TV for you. Does the bathroom have everything there you need?"

I rushed towards him and he couldn't help putting up one hand to protect himself, but I confined myself to slamming the door loudly.

From my window I had an incredible view into Central Park and I watched tiny couples strolling along the paths. I almost seemed to hear their words of love. While I undressed I told myself a couple of times: "You're not dreaming, you're in New York," and then I lay down on the bed, overcome by a fit of melancholy.

I was running my first New York bath when a valet entered without knocking. He placed a sheaf of flowers on the table. I was rooted to the spot like an idiot, stark naked, while the valet gaped at me appreciatively. I gave him the universally-acknowledged signal to clear out and grabbed the card that accompanied the flowers. I held it close to my nose so I could decipher the scrawl without finding my glasses. My head reeled.

I'm thinking of you. Marc.

I let out a howl of delight. Alexander dashed into my room shouting:

"What's the matter?"

He turned white when he saw I was in the nude. Without needing any further explanation, he scuttled back into his own room – after one dismayed look at the huge bouquet of flowers. I slipped starry-eyed into my bath, unable to concentrate and already immersed in fantasy.

I interpreted this banal message as a proposal, and I exulted, dreaming of making him jealous and ensnaring him in my cunning wiles. I would match his passion – a fury of lust in a New York bathtub. While caressing my sensitive breasts which were floating on the foam, I made my list of requirements for happiness. Two children, a house in Normandy with new vines, August holidays on the Côte d'Azure like the Belgians. I had only one desire – to be a normal girl just like other people, or rather, as you imagine other people are when they appear happy. I fell asleep in the bath and when I got out two hours later, cold and shivery, I'd caught a chill. I sneezed.

We dined at Trader Vic's, the Polynesian restaurant at the Plaza Hotel. Goraguine introduced me to his various American guests as "the new sexy French star". He added boastfully:

"She's my latest discovery."

I didn't like that, and what was more the dinner was a strained occasion, with interminable conversations conducted in an incomprehensible and mangled English: it's incredible how badly the Yanks speak English. From time to time one of the revellers would leer at me and Goraguine, winking, would burst into laughter. He explained that I was fifty per cent French, fifty per cent 'Made in USA'. The whole party cheered thunderously at that, and the fat guy to whom Goraguine was being particularly obsequious ordered a bottle of Dom Pérignon.

I drank to drown my woes, thinking about my flowers which would rapidly be wilting in that distant hotel room. I admired the way Marc had obtained my New York address the very day I'd arrived. Lost in my reveries, I spilt some lobster thermidor on to Goraguine's sleeve. He looked daggers at me and I took care to appear suitably contrite.

"Alexander, don't be horrid!"

He melted, squeezed my hand energetically, and grumbled: "Ah, you!"

Centuries later we rose from our seats and Goraguine shoved me towards Mr Big, murmuring:

"Smile and say thank you, Joy darling, *we're* being taken to Studio 54!"

I smiled gratefully and the big wheel whispered to me:

"Mam-zelle Joy, jay mapell Frank."

I immediately began calling him Frank and he was demonstrably delighted. We all piled into an even larger and more opulent limousine than the one at the airport and found ourselves wedged against one another. Goraguine perched on the folding seat opposite me and throughout the journey made revolting little movements of his lips which he must have thought appealing.

There was an incredible crowd blocking the way to Studio 54. The chauffeur hooted twice so that a muscle man could part the hysterical throng begging for the honour of being admitted to the trendiest New York nightspot. I entered the 54 on the arm of Frank Lorrimer, familiarly known in New York circles as King, and ran the gauntlet of envious glances from the extraordinary half-naked creatures who'd been waiting outside for hours.

The music, together with all those odours peculiar to nightclubs and composed of acrid perfumes, pot smoke and perspiration, at once assailed and intoxicated me. Frank passed me a huge joint which I smoked avidly, and everything started looking up. There were shaved heads; dyed and punkish hairstyles; a made-up Negro clad in green sequins; a fairhaired giant with an umbrella hat like something out of Rio carnival or the Medieval Mystery Plays; oiled breasts, pricks and cunts accentuated by figurehugging latex jeans, and everywhere that inevitable nervous restlessness produced by excess.

King Lorrimer introduced me to a disco star – Gary, handsome as a young god, a stevedore type with a skin smooth enough to make Elizabeth Arden herself jealous. He wore white sneakers and leather slacks so tight that I saw his prick move, squashed against his thigh. He embraced me as if we'd lived together for twenty years, then pushed me towards the twitching, gesticulating horde. He began dancing, rubbing himself against me. He wouldn't stop and I could hardly stand it any more: the champagne, the strobe lights which were making me dizzy, the earsplitting sound system, the jetlag, his too-tight jeans – everything made me feel as if I were cracking up once and for all.

However, we somehow struggled back towards the bar, where King Lorrimer favoured me with a sly wave and a jokey "Mam-zel Joy" while Goraguine sulked. Gary dragged me to one side whispering into my neck words I didn't understand, except for the often repeated 'love'. Outside, girls started screaming at him the moment they set eyes on him. I felt proud and quite impressed. A fusillade of flashbulbs caught us being a beautiful couple, and then Gary asked where I was staying. He signalled to his bodyguards, two rather cool heavies, and we were whisked off in a white Rolls, straight to the Park Lane.

I made as if to get out.

"Goodnight, Gary ..."

He looked at me ironically. Of course he was flirting with me, but all the same, I couldn't be unfaithful to Marc on the first evening with the first man I met, disco star or not, and not, what's more, in my room beside the flowers sent by the man I loved. Could I do a thing like that?

Yes, I certainly could.

CHAPTER NINE

To have a bad memory is to lead a double life. You can read the same book twice, cry over the same movie, revisit precisely the same landscape, greet the identical person, and love the same man with the pounding heart of someone discovering the unknown. "Delighted Madame to make your acquaintance," one might say formally – to an old schoolfriend, or "Hi Max you're putting on weight!" to a complete stranger confused with somebody else: the innumerable problems caused by inattention, carelessness, absent-mindedness or distraction pure and simple, are followed by the exhumation of unbidden memories, faithfully registered and reconstituted by one or another part of our bodies. Each aspect of our personality then seems to possess its own inbuilt memory.

The nose, for example, recalls certain scents which the brain is hard put to it to remember. Hands do not have good memories. Eyes remember everything. My heart and my sex organs never concur. They argue constantly. My heart has never forgotten anything since it first began to beat: it remembers the smallest detail, the most banal emotions, the first kiss in the Lycée playground, the birth of jealousy, absences, returns, lies. As for my sex, its memory is very limited. It's amnesiac, ungrateful and abstracted. It forgets the most intense sensations so rapidly that they sometimes resemble dreams. This is a frustrating dualism (and duel) – pounding heart and unmoved sex, or cold heart and sex on fire – which knows no respite and leads to neuroses, insomnia and a tearstained pillow. The list of bedmates grows, despair and chaos move in.

I lived through my first night in America like a curious

tourist won over at a glance. I drank bourbon, unable to stop myself looking at the telltale bouquets of flowers, even while Gary was nibbling my ears and whispering: "I want to suck your ass." I didn't understand, so he carried on and did it anyway. I was assailed by a long pointed tongue slithering into me while I was staring at the flowers – which surely drooped with shame as clumsy fingers ransacked me. I remained painfully distant, dry, foreign. He took me violently. I ought to have liked that, I should have come, but I had other things on my mind. I didn't understand what I was doing in the arms of this handsome, mechanical youth who wasn't even moving me as much as a marble torso I'd seen one day in a museum showcase.

He was by now showing signs of panic and I took pity on him. He was rather touching with his predictable, methodical thrusts, and his corny little mannerisms which he vainly hoped might break through my indifference. He had proudly offered me a sturdy erection, holding his prick out towards me as if it were a flower, his fingers gripping the twitching member which was the colour of the blood swelling those tiny snake-clusters of veins. I let my hand slide over his now slippery body, checking out his bulging muscles in the process, and then I grasped the warm hairy purse below the stiffened prick. His back arched, poor fellow, and taken by surprise he launched himself into me as if intending to break my back. Not wishing to seem frigid and trying to uphold the honour of France, I feigned a reassuring orgasm for myself as much as for him.

After the silence, the cigarette. The acrid scents drifting like mist in one's consciousness. Then the inevitable hand placed on breast or sex. And those words, the same in every language, which trail away in mid-air with questions unasked. I don't think Gary was fooled: he left in the small hours, noiselessly, taking care not to rouse me. I wasn't asleep, though. When the door closed behind him I sighed deeply and got up to kiss my flowers. They smelt so good, so strongly of France, Marc, and everything no sooner lost than missed.

The sun flooded my room. A waiter with a tray woke me. It was a huge, impressive tray, the very thing for a solitary banquet. There were frosted glasses and hot plates, buttered toast, soft boiled eggs, fresh orange juice, marmalade, grilled bacon, cut flowers, croissants and coffee. I bolted down this breakfast and lay back in bed to recover. Goraguine knocked and as he entered gave me a sharp look of martyred, long-suffering vexation. He said tensely:

"I hope you had a good time ..."

I wanted to write Marc a long letter, but after "Forgive me, my love" and two incoherent pages full of oblique hints, rhetorical questions and trailing ellipses I tore up my masterpiece. It was more fitting for my sublime words of love to turn into confetti lost in the muddy sewers of New York.

Wandering through Manhattan, Fifth Avenue, Madison and Park Avenues, Lexington and the rest, I found the same boutiques as in Paris, Rome or London. American shop staff gave me the sales pitch, and I bought some tee shirts, two or three sets of embroidered Mickey Mouse panties and a pair of photochromatic sunglasses. I returned exhausted to the hotel where Goraguine awaited me, very obviously undergoing seizures of anxiety.

"Joy darling, you're quite mad. What lunacy, going out all on your own in New York! It's crazy, you might have been mugged or raped, don't you realize ..."

Suddenly his eyes were goggling.

"And you went out ... dressed like that?"

Trembling, he pointed at my flimsy shift dress under which my braless breasts were, it must be admitted, clearly outlined.

"You're just asking to be raped! You must understand, Joy, I can't allow you to go out alone ..."

The next day he accompanied me. He absolutely insisted on getting me into an open carriage which progressed at such funereal pace that it caused traffic jams and prompted curses and dirty looks from sweating motorists. I felt ridiculous as Goraguine played guide, standing with one arm raised aloft to point out every building and every avenue, all the while delivering a nonstop running commentary. Dwarfed by the huge bulk of the concrete skyscrapers he resembled Napoleon facing the Pyramids.

At last the carriage dropped us off at a dreary shop where he usually bought striped longjohns and absurd tartan trews in which he could look even more appalling. We rounded off this memorable day with a visit to the World Trade Center. Everywhere I bought postcards by the dozen which I sent to all and sundry, to friends, to Alain, mother and even Marc, matching up message, view and addressee as best I could. I've always had a provincial tourist streak in me, and it invariably irritates my travelling companion, but when I sightsee I do see the sites. I never let anything distract me from my sole preoccupation: to hoard up souvenirs so as to recollect in tranquillity and tell stories about them later.

We would dine out with King and his friends virtually every night, in unusual restaurants taken for granted by New Yorkers. We would go along to Studio 54, where I was an accepted habitué, and then we would return to the hotel. Goraguine dogged my footsteps like a disgusting little basset hound, ready to hurl himself upon me the moment I relented. Several times I rang Marc in the middle of the night, but as soon as he answered I would hang up. I didn't know what to say to him. I only wanted to know that he was alive, and his sleepy, grumbling "Hello?" would reassure me. One evening, however, I could not resist.

"It's Joy, I'm in New York."

There followed a deathly silence.

"Good to hear from you. I think about you a lot, you know ..."

"Your flowers were lovely. Such a pleasant surprise," I babbled foolishly.

"You're just a little girl at heart." (Silence) "Do you like New York?"

"If we were together it'd be fine." I had capitulated. "But you're not here!"

Another silence.

"You realize ... I love you very much ..." (Silence) "I have to make it clear to you, though – I'm in love with Joelle ..."

My heart lay in smithereens over the carpet.

"At least you don't hate me for it, do you? I mean, Joy, – say something – Hello? Hello? You're not depressed, though? *Are you*?"

I'd have liked to reply with a neatly turned phrase full of impressive-sounding words, but all I could do was sniffle.

"Joy, I promise you we'll see each other again. I'll make love to you again, you know I can't do without it, yet there can't be anything *more* between us. You and I are beasts of the same species, wild creatures who can only meet in the forest, by night, without anyone surprising us."

Fury helped me hit upon a vocabulary of sorts, limited perhaps, but appropriate.

"Right, I get the message. And I draw the line at that. I'm going to live my own life. That clear? I'm not even going to think about you any more. I'll be loved all right, you stupid bastard, because I hardly have to lift a finger before some fabulous guy comes running ready to throw himself at my feet."

He burst out laughing.

"Men never *marry* girls like you, Joy. You don't exactly inspire marriage. Wait a while maybe, and in time you'll find your way and some sort of balance. You put people off, Joy – you're too attractive, too young, too free, too – well, somehow you scare them off, drive them away ..."

"You don't understand a thing, Marc. I think you're basically rather stupid ... You don't know me at all."

"I don't know you? My God, I'm sure you've already slept with plenty of men in New York, or am I mistaken?"

"It's all your fault," I screamed at him. "I'll throw myself at men, *any* man, and one fine day you'll regret it."

"I won't regret a thing, how can I, since I'm not in love with you? Can you understand that, Joy? I-am-not-in-love-with-you. You're wasting your life ... Pity ... Anyway. I'm sleepy. I'll ring you soon."

He hung up, and I stayed by the phone, shivering with cold and anger. I flung myself on to the bed, plumped three pillows round my head to shut off all noise, and fell asleep praying for death then and there, without my regaining consciousness, a coward to the end.

I went through a gloomy and workaholic phase. King Lorrimer, who was President of General Artists, engaged me to play various small parts in several modestly budgeted B movies. I toiled from dawn to dusk on some none too marvellous roles. By evening I would be dropping off to sleep in the taxi back to the hotel. I had no time for self-pity. King was wonderful to me. He never tried anything on with me because I think he considered me as a daughter, and that did me the world of good. I did have a bad depression one evening, and I confided in him.

"I feel so isolated and lonely, King darling. I can't stand the hotel, and I so need to feel at home ..."

King's spectacles blurred with emotion and the next morning I had a flat to myself, leased by the film company. I went wild with delight. I hurried round to King's home and hugged him as if he'd been my own father. He flushed in confusion and clasped my hand affectionately. I moved in the following week.

The block of apartments towered over Central Park at 70th Street. From my window on the nineteenth floor I looked out over the great shadowed mass of trees that was the Park. King and Goraguine turned up for the flat-warming with a crowd of strangers who made a pigsty of the newly-cleaned rooms.

I had quite a shock that evening. Goraguine introduced us to Joana, a voluptuous Puerto Rican with whom he was infatuated. They made a grotesque couple: she was tall, buxom and exotic, with sleek honey-coloured skin and black hair cascading to her buttocks, while he, bald and grey, seemed even more miniature and wizened by contrast.

I foresaw that this change in Goraguine's life was going to cause me some problems. And I was quite right. He no longer had any use for me and he let me know it. I rang him several times unsuccessfully until one morning I finally discovered that he had gone back to Paris with Joana. He never even said goodbye to me, nor, of course, did he pay me one penny of all the money he owed me. That evening, when I'd closed the kitchen door on my stack of dirty dishes, my thoughts drifted away from that isolated eyrie of mine – veering more and more between Lausanne and Paris, between Marc's arms and mother's. I made desperate efforts to forget but could not: each time I crossed the street and thought I saw someone who resembled him, my heart missed a beat, I would murmur "Marc!" and find I had to lean against a wall to recover.

Goraguine's departure succeeded in demoralizing me. I knew then that I had to start all over again, on every level, and that my stay in New York would turn out to be fruitless and disastrous. I was continuing to make blunders: I should probably have gone along with Goraguine and given him what he wanted. Had I undressed in front of him, slept with him – everything might have been quite different. Yet I was revolted by the very thought: no one has ever been able to restrain me from, or force me into, anything, not even Marc. All I had ever done in my life I'd done of my own volition. That was the only thing I valued, it was my consolation, and I was not about to change.

I met Steve Corleone, the twenty-five-year-old proprietor of a restaurant in Little Italy. He was the sort of man out of a romantic novel. Seductive, elegant and discreet, he fell for me the moment he saw me, and looked after me as if I were a backward child. He spent whole evenings sitting at my feet, in a sort of silent adoration: I'd never have thought such a thing possible.

Each night he would whisper tender words of love and when we slept together in the kingsized bed I had the impression that he was about to celebrate Mass. He embraced my body devotedly, religiously, with a scrupulous concern. He used to caress me so gently that one night I happened to fall asleep under his magic fingers. He would keep track of my slightest tremor, solicitous never to hurt me, and only entering me if I was almost on the brink, when I would myself guide him into me. He would take ages to come and even then would apologize for being too quick. He'd never let me handle him. Often I wanted to squeeze his prick, to play with it and suck it, because I have a physical urge to do this when lovemaking, but he would invariably pull away from me. I tried to explain to him that I needed to feel my lover's prick in my mouth and enjoyed

89

the sensation greatly. For me fellatio represented the logical expression of whatever it was that most attracted me to a man: to borrow and drink his sex was to accomplish a ritual which never caused me shame but, on the contrary, gave me a sense of calm fulfilment as soon as I received the seed in my mouth. He couldn't understand this. His long eyelashes would flutter and his handsome face begin to frown, then he would shut his soulful eyes, like Jesus with Mary Magdalene. And once again I'd be convinced that Jesus understood women far better than Steve Corleone whom I loved deeply for one whole week. To this day Steve is the only man I can talk about in the past tense, that irreversible syntax of time and death.

One day I could no longer bear the way he spurned my mouth, nor that he was making me fat, for each evening he always brought round cannelloni, fetucchini, tortellini, lasagne verde, spaghetti carbonara, chianti and so on. Reticence and avoirdupois, both at the same time, were just too much. So my Italian episode ended on the telephone one Sunday morning. It was raining. Steve had rung me to announce that he'd be calling for me, *mi amore*, at ten o'clock, in order to introduce me to his mamma.

"No, Steve," I answered. "Sorry."

"No? Why not? Why are you sorry?"

I replied calmly, with all the cruelty of detachment, that I'd had enough of spaghetti, of the mamma he talked about incessantly and of his own prudery. He hung up with a goodbye. *Arrivederci. Volare.*

The following night I fucked a friend of King, a man with greying temples and horn-rimmed spectacles who had invited me to his Manhattan penthouse on the top floor of a skyscraper suspended amid the dazzling lights. The next night I spent with someone else, and the night after that I stayed home drinking milk and guzzling popcorn. Around midnight I had a crazy impulse to go down into the street, where I headed slowly for the menacing undergrowth of Central Park.

I knew that death lurked behind those dark bushes and that some knife-wielding lunatic might jump out and rip me open, but I went on, terrified yet determined. Just as I was about to cross over to the edge of the Park I heard a squeal of brakes. An old green truck, dented and rusty, had pulled up behind me and a man in dungarees ran across to me. He was tall, powerfully built with broad shoulders. He had untidy fair hair and a blond almost gingery beard obscured his features. I was struck by his clear blue eyes, as limpid as my own. He smiled and somehow I felt I already knew him. Then he asked me various questions in a rather nasal voice. I didn't understand what he was saying, so I replied just in case:

"Je ne sais pas."

He laughed, revealing perfect teeth, and slapped his thigh.

"Vous êtes Française," he said in French with a terrible accent, "you don't know the danger. Not alone, *pas toute seule ici la nuit*. Killers, dan-geu-reu."

He stood facing me and indicated that I should climb into his cab. I did so, and by morning I knew the deserted streets and gutted buildings of New York, along with those automobile graveyards of Brooklyn. He had told me all about his city and shown me its secrets.

I waved goodbye to him – and imagined I had just met my father again.

CHAPTER TEN

One day I found in my letter box a coloured postcard – *Souvenir of Paris*, a pink envelope with a Lausanne postmark, and a cheque from General Artists. The postcard had only two words written on it: *When?* followed by a badly drawn heart and the signature *Marc*.

Mother had written three close-packed pages in her fine sloping hand. Once I used to decipher that writing with difficulty in my icy boarding-school. She went on about Lausanne and her leisurely life redolent of the scent of polish and camomile tea, extolling her happy retreat in Switzerland. I couldn't help recalling her brown, plump body which had attracted so many discerning men and which she was now offering that redhaired creep. She ended her letter with some trivial bits of advice I found touching. I sensed that we were gradually drifting apart and that she was ageing. When two people walk along the same street, one of them moving faster than the other, the one walking ahead always turns the corner in the end and moves out of sight for good.

That afternoon too, Margo rang me, with the usual stream of questions and laughter: "Joy, it's me darling. It's fine here in Paris and I've been thinking of you ... You know my love, I've met him at last, the man I've been waiting for all my life. He's taking me to the Bahamas ..."

"To the Bahamas?"

She began reminding me of that time when mother and I lived together at Meudon in a tall old house covered with ivy. Roses in the garden. Meals out on the sunwarmed terrace. Squared napkins and strawberry jam. The sort of things which made me feel bad, living as I was, nineteen storeys high in

Manhattan. I sniffed a couple of times, and her voice became concerned.

"What's the matter, Joy? Are you all right?"

"I'm quite all right, thanks," I replied. "Goraguine has gone back and I'm so lonely I could die. I can't stand it much longer."

"Joy, I know someone, a great friend of mine, who'll cheer you up. I'll call him straight away ..."

"Oh, yes, do," I sighed.

We said our goodbyes and I twice reminded her:

"I'm counting on you Margo, OK?"

I wandered round the apartment trying to occupy myself. It appeared I had twenty-nine dollars in change. By the time I'd counted it the phone rang again, and I was listening to a voice that sounded almost subterranean – deep, tough and gentle all at once.

"Good evening, I'm Margo's friend. Are you free this evening?"

Taken aback and somewhat distractedly, I said I was.

"I'll be at the front door of your building at ten sharp. Get dressed up and don't be late."

I spent an hour wondering what to do and tried ringing Margo again, but she had already gone out.

I lounged in the bath, splashing about for an hour or so and wondering about the owner of that extraordinary, almost terrifying voice. I slipped on a low-cut top and almost indecently tight black slacks, made myself up superbly – something out of the golden age of Hollywood – and sat and waited. I smoked nervously until the fatal hour approached, and at precisely ten o'clock was down in the foyer to see a shining Rolls draw up outside the main door.

I remained at the top of the steps. I fiddled with my handbag to give myself confidence while he, at the wheel of the Rolls, made no move. I did distinguish a dark and immobile silhouette rather like a crime thriller logo, consciously disturbing. Eventually the impassive mystery man opened the door. I went over to the Rolls leaning forward slightly so as to get a look at him, aware too that I must have resembled a prostitute picking up her customer.

He leaned over to the window with the nonchalant elegance of one no longer surprised by anything.

"Get in."

I slid into the car and was aware of a cocktail of different scents, a subtle mixture of the musky sharpness of leather, strong rolling tobacco and sandalwood essence. The dark and still taciturn profile was observing my silhouette closely and his long pale fingers toyed instinctively with the steering wheel. My heart beat faster as I thought I caught a nod of his head, just before he put the Rolls in gear and we moved off smoothly like a ship in the night. He smiled, teeth flashing in the shadow.

"Beauty is a promise of happiness."

My eyes widened at that. It was the most unexpected opening gambit I'd ever heard.

"Shakespeare should have known you, Joy."

I had no answer to that one, so he slowly repeated my name, several times, and with different intonations:

"Joy ... Joy ... Joy ..."

Turning into Fifth Avenue he was no longer in shadow and I had a good view of him at last. He drove expertly, without so much as a glance at me. I looked directly at him and in doing so felt some sort of relief. Not daring to break the silence I waited for him to ask me questions, but he was absorbed in driving the Rolls, which was now travelling over a bad road surface. I leaned my head back against the leather headrest and relaxed, extending my legs. I knew he would remain distant, detached. I shut my eyes, wishing in fact that he would behave like everyone else and talk or touch me – but he continued to be remote and indifferent. Each minute seemed to deepen the silence, and this oppressive silence was linking me to him. He stopped alongside a fence daubed with red paint and switched off the engine. I turned towards him and he looked at me at last. His eyes seemed to drill into me like lasers.

"My name is Bruce. You must forget what is troubling you. I know all about that. Don't say a word to me. Follow me and stay silent whatever happens. You must obey, *as you well know* ..."

94

He led the way to the door of a dark building. We crossed a courtyard, then he rang at a metal gate. I walked behind him trembling, doubtless with cold. We entered a warehouse lit by candelabra.

Heavy hangings rustled in the wavering light, draped from iron girders. A scarlet carpet covered the cement floor. Low lacquered tables were arranged symmetrically and covered with bouquets of dark flowers. In shadowy corners stuffed animals lurked: a panther with raised paw, a lioness with open jaws, and others I had no time to identify. A sudden unease overwhelmed me and I teetered on my high heels. Bruce had come back and was observing me impassively, as if he were sniffing out my fears. He lifted one of the hangings and pushed me into what resembled a sitting-room with a raised black dais.

A score of people were engaged in hushed conversation, the men mostly in dark suits and the women in long gowns. Ice tinkled in glasses, audible above the swish of silk and the sound of stifled sighs. Bruce took my arm and led me authoritatively towards a big Negress who scowled when she saw me. I could sense my lips quivering, because I was scared, but when I turned round Bruce had disappeared. The black woman seized my hand, giving me what she fondly imagined was a reassuring smile. Her hot palm pressed against mine and her expression softened.

"The black room and the red room. Bruce *insists* you see both. Starting with the red room."

She went over to a table and offered me a glass of champagne. "Drink this."

I drank the chilled liquid, trying to conceal that fact that my hands were shaking. Then at a sign from the hostess, I moved down some narrow passages leading to a room furnished with crimson velvet. Dim light reflected here and there off gilt and mirrors. Three women were seated in blood-red armchairs. I saw first a young Vietnamese with sleek, gleaming black hair. Her honey-coloured skin glistened with perspiration. Her nude body lay back relaxed against the armchair and her melancholy eyes lent fascination to a smile which exposed her pearly white teeth. Beside her sat a statuesque blonde, whose platinum mane fell over freckled shoulders bathed in a reddish glow. Her huge pendulous breasts were quivering under a tee shirt so taut as to be almost transparent. The lower half of her body was naked and her generous russet bush was fully exposed, pubic hairs extending to the tops of her thighs. Next to her, the third woman, who was darkhaired, seemed to be hiding her face: one hand was held over her brow and she wore large dark glasses.

I stopped uncertainly, and looked for my hostess. I was wondering about Bruce's disappearance and trying to fathom what this set-up was all about. The lights gradually dimmed to reveal three gilt-edged circular wall niches, illuminated from behind by bright, bluish spot-lighting.

These three niches were identical, each approximately the size of a large open book. Suddenly it started raining and I shuddered instinctively. I realized I was hearing rain without a drop of it falling on me: the din grew more deafening, then slackened to become finer and more distant. These exaggerated sounds were getting on my nerves and I developed gooseflesh, as if I'd been soaked in a cold shower. Just then shadows moved at the base of the niches and three objects appeared which I did not immediately distinguish. Blind as a bat, as usual, I approached them, only to find that each of the niches framed a man's prick, which dangled gently in front of my very eyes. Their owners' stomachs were pushed out and the short hairs shone slickly under the harsh spot-lights. As I imagined those three men concealed behind their niches, and like them awaited what was to happen next, a shudder ran through my body. I was fascinated by these patiently waiting members.

The Vietnamese woman rose first and approached the centre niche. She knelt down and I noticed that cushions had been laid in front of each niche. She cautiously put out her hand and grasped the long brownish organ hanging in front of her. The noise of rain again grew deafening. The young Eurasian gripped the member in her hand, abruptly tugging back the foreskin so as to lay bare the sizeable and swelling glans. In a few seconds the prick thus imprisoned attained impressive proportions: its complex knots of veins expanded below the taut skin and the whole prick began to resemble a snake ready to strike. I was unusually aroused: my temples broke out in a cold sweat while scalding heat seemed to course through my cunt. The young Vietnamese girl with her sad-eyed look held up the big stiff prick and her pointed tongue began to brush gently against its firm and rounded shaft.

I was shaken by the loud groan which the blonde woman behind me could not suppress. She got up and went to the first niche, from which another prick protruded, dropped to her knees and took the whole phallus into her mouth with a grunt. She engulfed it as though starving, working her head to and fro ardently. The hidden man's belly thrust forward further still, striving to sink its shaft deeper into that avid throat.

The third niche was occupied by a penis as red as the velvet walls, and a series of slow throbs were bringing it to erection. I approached it. I had to touch it, make it pulse between my fingers, and suck it into my parched mouth. The call was irresistible: nothing else existed except these fiery stems, these reddened roots that had to be appeased – because the rain's rhythm was becoming hypnotic, the night surrounded us, isolated us from the rest of the world, and I needed this anonymous cock. My parted lips would soon close over the firm shaft, waiting for its violent discharge to be drunk drop by drop. I knelt, seized the prick, which smelt of musk and incense, and began to fellate it as it twitched and slithered between my hands with alarming gentleness. I closed my eyes, taking it in deeper, possessed by the frenzied desire to make it come before the others: I wanted it to be the first to die along my tongue. I sucked as hard as I could, discovering that I had reserves of hitherto unsuspected strength.

The Vietnamese was bobbing her head, her hair flying everywhere and tears brimming at her eyelashes. Then she pulled back abruptly so that the enormously distended prick could spurt in full view under the bluish light. Her tongue strained to a point, its tip tapping furiously just below the glans, which contracted then pulsed to spray pearls over her hair. It spattered her neat little nose and curved eyelashes with liquid ivory, and, lower down, scattered thick white droplets upon her saffron-coloured breasts. Lips encircling it again, she then slaked her thirst, slowly swallowing whatever remained to well forth.

I speeded up my mouthing, my nails lightly scratching the swollen root which twitched in response. A copious tide flooded my mouth and overflowed, trickling through my lips and down my chin to drip on to my heart like acid. The rest of the warm fluid oozed down my throat and into the very depths of me. I had reached the bottom of the abyss by drinking this thick seed to the last drop. The rain suddenly ceased.

Hands took hold of me gently and bore me through the shadows and past the lights. I felt humiliated not through having succumbed to my desire, but because I had participated in the ritual. The mysterious Negress offered me an iced drink, with a smile in which I thought I detected both amusement and surprise. She undressed me carefully, placing my tunic top over an armchair. My breasts felt a slight draught and then, instinctively, I shut my thighs tight, for my cunt felt sopping wet.

"Now, come to the black room."

She nodded, as if to say: "You must – Bruce decided you should." She swathed me in a black silk veil embroidered with silver and led me into a long chamber lit by a baleful purple radiance.

The room had three reclining chairs in it, each of studded black leather. One end of each chair was pointing towards a dark niche, and arranged in such a way that the occupant would lie back with the upper half of his or her body in this darkened room while the lower half, from the waist down, projected into the forbidding darkness. I knew all too well, then, the nature of the magic ritual which would ensue, whose culmination would be the brutal cure for those capricious yearnings which constantly stirred within my cunt.

I was about to offer my sex to an unknown mouth concealed in the darkness. The controller would become the victim, the executioner was to suffer martyrdom, and justice would be done. I lay full length in the torture chair, the lower half of my body plunged in darkness. I tilted my head back in a state of shock now that I was actually playing out the fantasies which had plagued me since adolescence. I remembered how I used to dwell upon one particular moment during those fevered nights, when a mouth, thrust beneath my raised skirt, would explore that streaming wet orifice, cool tongue upon blood-filled tiny bud, lecherous snake nibbling the juicy button till the spasm of pleasure burst free.

The little Vietnamese girl had slipped behind me. She placed her face upon mine, upside down, and her lithe tongue licked my lips while I savoured on her spittle the musky aftertaste of the pleasure she had just imbibed. My hands found a full, long-nippled breast, brushed against her clearly outlined little ribcage, glided over a curving buttock and finally reached the rough pubic lace fringing the lips of her spicy sex, so bitter and oily and like some carnivorous flower contracting at my caress. My fingers sank into the moist membranes, catching like little hooks inside the silken interior until the Vietnamese girl pushed in my whole hand, while she shook and quivered in her spasm, her vagina throbbing like a displaced heart.

A sudden paroxysm coursed through me like an electric current, diverting my attention from the tender caress of the Eurasian girl now licking my cheeks. My sex was being assailed by a supple, forceful organ which was dabbing at my clitoris and parting my labia brusquely. The tongue was working its way into me liked a crazed butterfly or some twisting, wriggling snake. I squirmed in the chair as if I were being whipped, and bit my fist so as not to cry out, thus preserving the unnatural silence. I stared intently at the black pearls sewn on to the velvet hangings as if I might recognize in them the tears of my own pleasure. The tidal climax swirled inexorably around my inflamed ridge, a tidal wave that dashed at last deep within my womb. I came violently into that gluttonous mouth lapping me up.

In the charged darkness of the black room I wept, while the young Vietnamese girl laid her head against my stomach. Her eyes gleamed like stars and I recalled her silent cry; that mouth opening upon pleasure I shall never forget. I was crying however, at having gone beyond the limits of my desires. What was left for me now that I had gone as far as I could and perhaps further still?

I could not justify my orgasm by talk of love, tenderness, passion or even desire. I had been manipulated from within, as it were: my entire nervous system had been sensitized, and the giddy paroxysm which had overcome me had simultaneously shown me horizons I never suspected and the difficulty I would henceforth encounter in attaining them.

CHAPTER ELEVEN

Who could possibly be interested in the trials of some wretched girl alone in a hostile and complex city? Who will even want to read to the end of this confession which burdens me so, and distresses me even today, long after the events described? Already I can imagine irreversible judgements, pitiless criticism. Here I am stripping myself quite naked: I exhibit myself more shamelessly in words than I could ever do by exposing my body. From the outset I accept indifference and lack of interest. Yet I know some readers of this book will recognize themselves here, since my story with all its naivety and banality, and for all its simplistic or shameful aspects, is essentially a love story many have lived: the account of those secret loves no one reveals, which in the bitterness of failure one keeps to oneself. So much the worse for bourgeois ladies who judge me by bourgeois standards, or for sluts who condemn me out of hand. It is those others who interest me, women with passionate natures like my own – poor creatures! – who can confide in no one because no one will listen to them, because no one can spare the time.

My contract with General Artists expired. King promised to help me should I need anything at all, but he did not put any further work my way. He smiled paternally at me: "Joy, you'd do better to return to France."

I nodded and walked off down Park Avenue, eventually reaching my apartment after a long detour. There I shut myself in. I was trying to save money, and whenever there was no dinner invitation I'd buy a hamburger and sit in front of the TV till I fell asleep, sucking my thumb and nuzzling against a cushion that had the texture and smell of mother's angora jumpers long ago.

I saw Bruce again several days after our meeting. He took me out to dinner at Palm's on Second Avenue. I devoured a large lobster and got rather drunk on Californian champagne, for I felt happy and relaxed because somebody cared about me and was being attentive, gentlemanly and polite. Afterwards he held my hand and opened the door of the Rolls for me. I saw him walk round the car, frowning slightly, his curly hair ruffled by the breeze. And I felt a surge of desire for him, just as he was, standing in the squalid New York night, so that when he sat beside me I rested my head on his shoulder, whispering his name. The Rolls swept through the streets full of potholes, amid the jets of steam issuing from the glistening asphalt, then he turned to me and said:

"I understand, Joy. *Me too.*"

We went to Regine's. There was Dom Pérignon, a reserved table, a deferential head waiter. The rather strained ambiance was accentuated by the sight of many very young girls accompanying elderly men who seemed to be there for distraction rather than genuine enjoyment.

"Bruce, let's leave. I'm depressed."

He looked gravely at me.

"I'll call you a taxi."

I felt deeply humiliated and rose to my feet just as a couple passed, lit momentarily by a wan beam of light. The very attractive girl in the maroon dress, with curly shoulder length hair and a charming mischievous grin was Joelle.

I thought I'd pass out as pain stabbed through me, for I was afraid I'd see Marc. But the man with Joelle was fairhaired and wore thick spectacles. Bruce caught my stricken look and leaned towards me:

"What's the matter?" he enquired anxiously.

"Nothing, Bruce. Nothing, memories ..."

He looked at Joelle and filled a glass of champagne. She moved forward slowly, searching for a free table, then she saw me. A dazzling smile.

"How marvellous, Joy! What luck!"

I adore her smile – it's quite inimitable – and I like her eyes too. In fact I really like this girl who has caused me unhappiness.

We talked for ages, standing there being jostled by boring men, for we had much to discuss. I wanted to introduce her to Bruce, but he had suddenly left, so we sat down at the vacant table. She informed me she was on a fortnight's business trip to New York, and with an eloquently contemptuous wave indicated the superior fellow escorting her. He joined us, sitting down with a brisk nod at me which passed for Good Evening. We chatted quite a while without managing to thaw him out. This dreadful person was apparently suffering from terminal boredom.

"He's head of the New York office of my magazine," she whispered to me, rolling her eyes in mock terror, "and I don't know how to get rid of him."

Our gossip continued for hours, until the escort could no longer suppress a yawn. Joelle then let him have it.

"I'm really sorry, we're talking about such boring things, aren't we ... You must be tired, surely? Shall we see each other again tomorrow?"

The bigwig rose to his dignified feet, kissed our hands, arranged to see her at the office at noon, bade us goodnight and disappeared into the shadows, flanked by two flunkeys. We laughed hysterically and drained the bottle of champagne by way of tasting our freedom. I watched Joelle liven up and as she smiled my heart swung between hate and affection. I already knew all about her life, how she loved travel and the twin sister she rarely saw, who would one day, poor kid, make what's called a 'good' marriage! Joelle loved the countryside but said she never spent enough time in it, and men too, provided they were very dominant types. I couldn't restrain myself.

"And Marc?"

Her face fell. She looked glumly down at her glass.

"Don't mention him to me. He rings me up three times a day. It's awful, that over-possessive sort of love ..."

She didn't realize that her words were tearing me apart, nor that I was making heroic efforts to stop myself bursting into floods of tears.

"He's wonderful, but I just don't have the same view of love. Every so often I need him, but if I see too much of him I can't bear it. He's too nice, he does everything I like, everything for my pleasure, but I can't stand it. If I'm away from him for a few days he gives me the whole drama – exaggerated jealousy and all that scene. Anyhow Joy, I've met another man who attracts me, I'm not quite sure why, but I do know I'll probably marry him. Marriage is a kind of conclusion: I'm not too keen on passionate dramas, you know, and with this other man I won't be running the risk of going through all that again ..."

"Won't you see Marc any more?" I asked.

"Occasionally, for – look, I'm not the faithful type. When I was eighteen I had my once-in-a-lifetime great love. His name was Didier. I'm ashamed to recall it, but when he went off to work in the morning I used to ring up another man to get him to make love to me in a bed that was still warm. And yet I really loved Didier to distraction ..."

"But given all that, aren't you and Marc pretty compatible just the same?" I enquired hypocritically.

She looked at me in embarrassment.

"It's fine, but he loves me too much, if you understand me. He makes love almost too well, *too correctly*. With the other guy things are different. I'm no longer up on the pedestal, I'm just an ordinary woman. He doesn't treat me with any special consideration. I'm loved casually, mistreated even. I know it's silly, but that's what excites me ..."

That was the sentence which trailed off endlessly into a night I no longer understood. Everything was muddled: here was this girl Marc loved, who didn't love Marc and whom I loved (and why not?) like Marc did. I watched her as she talked about her childhood during the Algerian war, holidays in the Savoie, the family she really never knew – all those postcards and clichés. Her lips would tremble, along with her nicotine-stained fingertips, whenever she lit a cigarette. And she would look at me with those lustrous eyes of hers which always unsettled me.

"Joy, don't go off and leave me tonight. Can I come and sleep at your place?"

"Yes," I said, more than a little surprised. "Yes, of course. Come on, let's go."

I took her hand and we went out on Park Avenue to be met by a gust of wind. We linked arms tightly and walked up Fifty Ninth to Fifth Avenue, which runs alongside Central Park. She began talking about her mother whom she seldom saw, talking so seriously and tenderly that I could have hugged and kissed her on the spot, there and then in front of General Motors Building, among the whores soliciting tourists. Whenever I'm fond of someone I have to tell them so – that's how I am. Marc could take a running jump – *she* existed and *she* was there beside me.

When she entered my apartment, she exclaimed:

"How lovely! I really like the carpet. And how about that, was that your idea?"

She seemed almost to enter into people, even things, somehow permeating them, and once that happened her presence was there for good. She asked me where her room was and I burst out laughing.

"There's only one bedroom, you know, and one bed!"

She gave me a funny look, then her incredible smile.

"Fine!"

She shut herself into the bathroom and I sank into my not-so-comfortable armchair, feeling as depressed as I had on the day mother packed me off to a holiday camp. The bathroom door opened and she appeared, nervous and nude. I found her very attractive, tall and lissom, with beauty spots all over her body. She asked me shyly if she could go to bed. I stared without answering at her pale slender legs, her pubic triangle so much darker than mine, and her rounded breasts with their erect nipples. Then I nodded quietly.

"Yes, of course."

I went into the bathroom then and began behaving as if preparing to sleep with a man. I stared at myself in the mirror, wondering if I were in my right mind. I'd never made love to a woman, not because it didn't attract me, but because I'd never felt the need to do so. Nor had the opportunity ever presented itself. I guessed that something serious was starting up between us both, and I was scared that she would reject me. I felt ill at ease. For the first time I was cast in the role of the adversary, taking the man's part, and I finally understood what a man goes through, the night he sleeps with a new girl for the first time. I put on some 'Jungle Gardenia', and came out boldly, breasts jutting, and with my nicest smile. She had switched off all the lights and I advanced towards the dark bed, with the curious sensation that I had turned into Marc and was about to make love to her just like he did. She had curled up in a corner of the bed – my favourite corner, in which I would masturbate or cry to myself – right down beneath the bedclothes and as far away from me as possible.

After a moment she turned and looked at my body, white against the dark sheets.

"You're lovely, you know."

I turned over between the cold sheets and stretched out slowly in order not to alarm her. I seemed to lie there for an age, not daring to move, scarcely to breathe, in a state of suspended animation, awaiting that one movement. She was still looking at me, her head raised slightly and her smile no longer so carefree. I thought I heard her heart pounding, even from the other side of the bed. The darkness in the bedroom had a bluish quality and her body had merged with the night, but with an effort I could just discern her eyes staring into mine. They were bright, yet I could not tell whether tears had made them sparkle so: I would truly have liked her to weep with me, both of us crying together.

I turned over again with a sigh, extended an arm and found that my hand was now resting on her hip. She trembled, but remained in the same position. I bit my lip. Her skin felt smooth, very warm and a little moist. Slowly I unclenched my hand. Its fingernails tickled her stomach, which contracted. My hand then moved downwards, followed the curve of a buttock, reached her thigh and found refuge in the hollow of her knee. Very gently I moved the hand back up her tense body and the higher it went the warmer her skin felt until suddenly I stopped – at her burning-hot lips. Her body went rigid. I avoided touching her sex and slid my hand over her flat, athletic belly. Then my hand slipped up to her breasts.

She whispered "Joy", but I did not answer, sitting up instead and moving over to kiss her. My tongue parted her lips and I kissed her as I'd never really known how to kiss a male lover. For the first time a kiss meant something to me, was no longer a habit. Her mouth had a faint aroma of aniseed like a field in the sun, warm yet cool at once, and now I was taking her as a man would have done. I was a man, I gripped her shoulders and my mouth brushed her cheeks and ears. I lightly kissed her eyelids and her nose too, tenderly. This is what love was like, then, beyond the pale, behind that forbidden barrier.

She moaned when my mouth moved over her nipples: these I teased, the way I like being tormented, while I stroked her thighs and she whimpered tiny cries which drove me wild. When my lips found the concealed spices and bitter-sweet incense of her cunt, she tried to stifle her groans by biting at her fists. Then I brushed my pursed lips against her half-open labia, let my tongue press the hardening pearl, and sucked at it until she thrust back my head with both hands. I resumed, plunged wet-mouthed as deep as I could into her pulsing cleft and raised my head to tell her: "You know it's the first time I've done this."

"Me too," she replied.

I lapped her then like a little dog, persistently, while her nails dug into my neck. She was shaking all over when her climax caught her, sudden as a whipcrack. I heard her spasmodic gasps as my face was drenched in a copious moisture, that hot flow of juice from an exotic fruit which I adored. I fell back, legs open, all of me open and aching, yet I didn't want her to touch me: I needed to possess her, be in her, direct her pleasure by the movements of my loins. When I felt her hand slyly feeling for me, however, I spread my legs still wider. She parted my labia and dug into me, nails scratching me, delving cruelly deep. Spread-eagled, I screamed with pain and pleasure, taken, for this intense moment, by surprise. It was as if our bodies were both steeped in thick, musky oil; our legs were entwined, breasts crushed against each other, sodden hair thrashing and flailing like the thongs of a whip. My cunt contracted around her hand and I fell back into a wild, dizzying rhythm until I passed out. Calm returned. After our irregular gasping breaths, like sudden lightning flashes in the dark night, there was an oppressive silence.

After a long time I got up, feeling very thirsty. She lay there quite motionless. I made her drink, holding her head up for her as if she were injured, and making sure that not a drop of this somehow precious liquid escaped her parched and swollen lips. I lay beside her and she laid her head between my thighs, talking so quietly to my cunt that I couldn't overhear her whispers. She embraced me generously, planting tender kisses on my bruised stomach. I burrowed close against her.

"We won't say anything stupid, will we? Let's just accept what we've just done."

She placed a finger on my lips to interrupt me.

"I'd like more of that, Joy."

I invaded her body, softly then violently. Her mouth browsed over me at leisure, and under this patient unhurried mouth I melted like a child and forgot all my fears. She was Marc, since she was making love to me.

I don't know how long this lasted, but dawn had banished the shadows inhabiting the bedroom, and Joelle looked peaceful and relaxed when I awoke.

A police car passed, its siren screaming. Death wakes early in New York.

Sunshine caught her hair as she slept on, cradled against my breasts. Her lips were slightly parted. I noticed some drops of vaginal fluid upon her thighs, like dew. She was shivering, as if cold.

The next day everything had changed. The atmosphere was grim and grey as Halloween. We avoided looking at each other and when we did so inadvertently she would force herself to smile. I'd have liked to kiss her but I knew she would have pushed me away, saying "No, not now." The coffee was as bitter as I felt, deep down, while the silence grew unbearable: how awful it all was, after such a beautiful night. We had woken early, and I was now dreading the moment when she'd have to leave. Then suddenly and for no obvious reason she relaxed. She came and sat beside me, asked me for a light, and I held out my lighter for her. She gave me an awkward sidelong glance as she was lighting her cigarette.

"Joy ... Marc told me everything, you know. He said you were in love with him, and even maintained that it was quite unreasonable. He said he loved you too, but in his own way, if you understand me. Joy, he's just like other men: the moment you get really involved he runs a mile."

"I'm not involved, nor am I running after him," I replied curtly. "I haven't the time."

"You're too sincere, you talk too much. You need to keep your mystery, Joy. With men like him, especially, one mustn't be encouraging or make them feel too sure of themselves ..."

I no longer wanted to answer her.

"Joy, what you did last night was because of Marc, wasn't it? A sort of revenge? Is that it?"

I was horrified. I felt betrayed, stripped naked, spurned. I could have admitted that I'd really felt attracted to her and still was, but what was the point? I shrugged, assuming an obstinate and sullen expression. She knelt in front of me, tenderly stroking my hair. She brushed my lips with a fingertip.

"Joy, you're irresistible. I didn't want to, last night, but I was attracted to *you* too."

A moment later, she whispered:

"You give too much, you give everything. You're too fragile and loving. You should get tough, take the offensive ..."

I shook my head despairingly. She didn't understand at all.

"I can't. I can't change. It's not my fault, I'm built that way. My heart's made of cardboard, it goes soggy the moment someone cries on it."

"I know, I know," she said, her eyes glistening.

She left and did not come back again. I found a blue envelope in my letter box and read it, trembling.

Joy: I'll never forget what happened, it'll be our secret, just between ourselves. But life goes on. You're in love with Marc, and everything's too complicated for me. Probably for you too. I ask you, please, not to say a word to Marc. Love and kisses, Joelle.

The night after that depressing day, Bruce invited me to dine with him at a celebrated restaurant in Chinatown. The place was down a dark sidestreet and consisted of one long room with gilt panelling and about ten tables. Tiny young girls were silently waiting on the few customers. They brought us delicate spiced dishes, exquisitely flavoured, and bobbed timidly each time Bruce addressed a word to them. Since I've never been able to keep a secret, I told him about the fabulous night I'd spent with Joelle.

"I thought as much," he replied with a faint grin.

I really liked asking him questions because he was never at a loss for an answer. We talked for a long time and the conversation invariably returned to the subject of travel.

"I don't enjoy travelling," I confessed to him. "It destroys my equilibrium. Yet the day I no longer expect anything, I know I'll take off, go far away. I've often fantasized that one morning I'll find an air ticket to some faraway place. Just one ticket. A single, to the unknown."

"A really tempting situation. But are you sure you'd be brave enough? Would you truly decide to leave?"

"If it came to it, yes, of course. As of now, though, no one's taken me up on it. I've told every man I've ever known about that dream, and so far no one's ever felt the urge to whisk me off, just him and me on some desert island ..."

"Men are idiots," he replied. "Do you like passion fruit?"

I suggested to Bruce that he came up to my apartment for a goodnight drink, since I didn't want to be on my own again.

"I never have that one last drink," Bruce replied slowly.

As the Rolls glided off after dropping me back, I took the decision to return to Paris. King Lorrimer was the first to know, and he remarked: "I understand, Joy. That's fine," without any undue show of regret. I rang mother in Lausanne, and she listened to what I had to say before commenting:

"What a pity I can't see you when you get back, it would have been nice to meet up. But we're off to St Moritz with friends. When I get back, though, I promise we'll spend a few days together."

Humiliations, disappointment, failure and return. Bruce wanted to make one of my dreams come true, however, and on the day of my flight he took me to Disneyland. A plane whisked us off at dawn to that world of fairies and magic animals. I saw pirates, rabbits and blonde dolls on a roundabout, Mickey and Donald dancing in the streets of the enchanted village – and was thrilled by it all. I was an eight-year-old again, I believed in everything, a happy toddler eating toffee apples, while Bruce went off to buy me a plastic watch on whose dial Mickey's nodding head told the time. "It's time to go," he kept saying and I felt close to tears.

I arrived late at Kennedy Airport, clutching my crumpled tourist class ticket and my heavy suitcase, and having to race through the necessary formalities. The Air France hostess glowered at me and I had difficulty finding an empty seat. I can confirm that there's quite a difference between Concorde and a cheap package flight. It's longer and not so pleasant nor so comfortable. And as for those plastic meals on plastic trays!

A tall man wearing glasses would stroll from time to time through the First Class section where he was sitting, past my seat. As he did so he kept giving me meaningful imploring looks. When the woman sitting beside me had temporarily vacated her seat he immediately took it.

"Apologies for disturbing you, but I'd be very happy if you'd have dinner with me one day when you're at a loose end. Allow me to give you my card. My name's Henri, and that phone number always finds me. Should you chance to be free one evening, bear me in mind. You won't regret it ..."

I tried to look as unpleasant as I could, scowling and baring my teeth.

"And why won't I regret it?"

The stranger smiled delightedly.

"But Mademoiselle, every woman has her price, and I'm prepared to pay whatever price is necessary. One should always know how to assess the rare at its true worth. What's your price?"

I blushed, rose to my feet, and headed for the toilets with as much dignity as I could muster.

CHAPTER TWELVE

I hardly recognized Paris. The streets had become narrow and buildings had shrunk. Everything seemed smaller, and this was both sad and comforting. Americans are more far-sighted, hence they build taller buildings. The taxidriver who drove me to Avenue de Breteuil wore a beret, his cab reeked of garlic and he flashed lecherous glances at me through his driving mirror: Vive la France!

Parking my heavy suitcase on the pavement, I went to the concierge's cubbyhole: for once, of course, she wasn't there. I hung about for an age in the hallway, dropping with exhaustion. Already I was missing New York, King and especially Bruce. I needed a hot bath, and plenty of time on the telephone letting everyone know I was back – Joy was back, alone and desperate for music, for distraction to exorcise the depression that ruined her days and made her nights a hell.

The concierge arrived, hobbling along.

"Goodness, what a surprise! But Mademoiselle hasn't changed a bit, she's just the same!"

She confided that she had won on the state lottery:

"Seven thousand francs, can you imagine!"

She insisted relentlessly on showing me the winning ticket, which she'd had photographed.

"Touch it, go on, it'll bring you luck!"

And like a complete idiot, touch it I did, just to speed things up.

"I'd like the keys, please."

Mother had only one pair of keys for the flat, and these I'd entrusted to the concierge so she could water the plants.

"The keys?" she repeated in astonishment.

"Yes. The keys."

"But – didn't you know?"

"No," I managed to answer, very weary by now, "I don't know."

"Your mother's let the place to her friends from Switzerland. They moved in on Monday. So you don't have another set of keys ..."

I began to cry.

"But what's all this about, it's my home, why's mother let my apartment? Anyway, I spoke to her yesterday and she never mentioned a thing about it to me ..."

"She thought you were going to stay in New York, poor lady. You must understand her point of view, Mademoiselle."

I picked up my case again and walked off under the plane trees lining the Avenue. I was frantic, for I had nowhere to live any more, no money left, and nobody was expecting me. I stopped by a phone booth. Out of order. I went into a bar, put down the case and ordered a white coffee and some bread and butter. I took two jetons and went downstairs to the cramped and stale-smelling phone cabin.

I rang Alain's number – well, what choice did I have? – as I deciphered various graffiti. Populist erotica, as depressing as usual: will one ever read on these poisonous walls inscriptions that are imaginative rather than disgusting? I knew those sordid comments and boastful drawings by heart almost before the phone began to ring in that doll's house where I wouldn't have minded living. There was no answer from Alain and I hung up. I rang Marc, very apprehensively. One ring, two, three.

"Hello?"

"Hello, Marc? It's me, Joy."

I plunged in at the deep end:

"I've just got back to Paris."

I fell silent and he did not answer. I could hear some faint music in the background, apparently in rhythm with my heartbeat.

"Come over. I'll be waiting for you."

114

I smiled, and if he'd been able to see that smile, I told myself, he'd certainly have thawed.

A taxi took me over to his flat, by a route unfamiliar to me. I fantasized that I was arriving in Belgrade or Budapest, some forbidding and hostile town where a stranger waited for me in an empty apartment whose walls were a weathered yellow. I placed my big suitcase on the red staircarpet and rang the bell. He opened the door with one sweeping movement as if he'd been watching me from behind it. He said "Joy" and pulled me to him. I smelt cachous and lavender as he kissed me on the lips for a long, long time – a tender, sweet, sad exploratory kiss, and I think a sincere one. He then led me inside.

"Quickly Joy, come on in."

He pushed me into the sitting-room, holding me by the waist, and almost picked me up and deposited me on the settee. He gave me a drink as I watched him through my tired eyes. I had a lump in my throat, and I told myself I must not say anything stupid or be the first to make a false move: I hoped in fact that *he* might, so I could reproach him with it later. He'd brought over a bottle of champagne as I sprawled across the settee. This then was happiness, the unexpected, a sudden shock. The tall mirror told me I was looking good, more attractive than ever – then I saw the lipstick-stained cigarette butts in the ashtray. A woman had had to leave because of me, a woman weaker than I: this I considered a kind of triumph and I was rapturous.

I told him about my life in New York, the people, my apartment, my work there. Proudly I showed him copies of *Harper's, Vogue, Playboy*.

"You're a star," he whispered, impressed.

He held me in his arms and began caressing my breasts.

"Did you have lots of lovers?"

I pulled a face and did not answer him. He frowned and looked somewhat crestfallen.

"And did *I* ask *you* that?"

"Look, I'm dog-tired. Been working too hard. I need a holiday."

I let him go on talking for a long time and then asked:

"And how's Joelle?"

He lowered his head, at the same time, making a little dismissive gesture as if to say "It's all too complicated to explain." I guessed he was unhappy. I'd have done anything to see him smile. I'd have liked to whisk Joelle out of my pocket, saying to him: "Here she is then, I've brought her along for you."

Probably no one can understand that, yet I'm quite right. When you love somebody, there are no half measures. I'm a Leo, and that's how Leos are, they take things to the limit, even if it kills them. I so want to be needed that if someone calls on me for help I'll drop everything, forget all other obligations – because at that moment nothing matters except to demonstrate how indispensable I am, and this in itself is a form of neurosis – masochism or megalomania. I may be crazy, but when Marc lowered his head in submission because he was on the defensive, I just couldn't let him stay like that. I took his face between my hands and kissed his eyes, praying that some day he would cry over me. I murmured:

"Marc I'm here, I love you more than anyone ever will, because after my love everything else will seem petty and meaningless."

His expression changed, became set. I had just committed a fatal error. He sat up, smiling and asked me slyly:

"Why have you brought a suitcase?"

I felt utterly humiliated. I stammered something he didn't understand, and which I didn't either.

"Are you intending to stay?" he added.

He undid his shirt, poured me out some champagne which I sipped, trembling, and then he dimmed the lights. He stared at me with an ironic glint in his eye.

"Come here," he said. "Leave your suitcase and come and pay your rent."

I never imagined that a weekend could last so long. We ate, slept, drank and laughed in a tangle of crumpled sheets. I can't recall how many times Marc made love to me, but my pleasure grew ever more intense. Marc continually seemed to be caressing me and whispering tender words: "You're like a

116

little nest, you're rain, you're a cloud, you're so beautiful I never tire of your beauty, you're the most beautiful woman I've ever had ..."

Sometimes he would part my legs and gaze, reflectively, at my shamelessly open sex, then he would brush his lips or chin against it until I was writhing and jerking, ready for him to enter me. He would take me violently, eager to provoke the grimace of pain I could never suppress, then he would remain motionless. I felt invaded by this foreign body throbbing inside my cunt, this alien object, which became harder still whenever I slowly moved my pubis or whispered those words he loved to hear. He'd close his eyes then: he always shut his eyes when fucking, and I knew every expression on his face as it contorted near orgasm. I knew each vein pulsing at his temples, and that wisp of hair that covered what I dubbed his little bald patch. He'd remain immobile for as long as he could and then deliver a brutal thrust which would hurt me because I wasn't expecting it, and then another, still more violent. Then he would stop, make me wait until I was begging him and crying out words which became beautiful because he liked hearing them. I'd stroke his back, move right down beneath his thighs, leaving a fierce red trail; sometimes I'd pummel him with my clenched fists and my nails would scratch him cruelly, trying to cause him pain. Then he'd rage and hammer at me with incredible strength, his body twisting so as to plaster itself against mine, trying to work his way a few millimetres further, to penetrate the very depths of my body. Then he would withdraw, asking me hoarsely to beg him for it, and I'd groan: "Marc, please, for God's sake come back inside me, I need you in me ..."

He'd make me come then in a matter of seconds, welding us together until I collapsed. He disliked coming inside me, but immediately I recovered from my orgasm he'd pull out and I'd take his prick in my mouth, impregnated as it was with my own scents, leading him on carefully to climax. Obsessed with giving him an orgasm even more powerful than my own, I'd concentrate on the movements of my lips and the suppleness of my tongue, taking him far down into my throat until he finally let go, groaning in climax as if he were ill, reaching that pitch of intensity where pleasure resembles pain. I would drink him again, swallowing each gradually less copious spurt, while his face changed: his frowning expression relaxed, his brow became smooth again, and life's tensions seemed not to have left their mark on him.

The time passed slowly – occasionally an hour or two might go by without a word being spoken. He read a lot, lying on the settee, and whenever he looked up he invariably seemed surprised to find me watching him, motionless. He'd frown at this.

"Why are you looking at me?"

"I'm not," I would lie.

We went out to a restaurant and to the cinema. In the middle of the night we drove off in his car for mystery tours that took us to Sèvres and Meudon. We passed the house in which I lived with mother when I was a timid little schoolgirl. In those days the garden was alive with bees, and I recalled the red and white square cloth on which I spilt some jam: mother had been angry with me, which broke my heart, since I saw so little of her and the time seemed too precious to quibble over a jam stain on linen. The house had been sold and repainted. It had lost all its enchantment, its special atmosphere, and was now just another suburban villa.

I had not even unpacked my suitcase. It was waiting for me in the hallway, standing against the wall as if to mock: *This isn't your home, you'll have to leave here sometime* ... Marc didn't want me to cook, and I was categorically banned from doing housework. A Spanish woman came in to clean every morning and she looked on me as an enemy. As soon as she left I revelled in being on my own – and would then start exploring Marc's secret world.

I opened wardrobe doors to reveal a succession of hanging suits, piles of jumbled shirts, ties astride a loose metal rod. I never touched a thing, though. I simply wanted to look through his belongings. I took in the smallest details. How he stubbed out his cigarettes. All the things he tended to do mechanically on his return each evening. He would head for some piece of furniture and empty his pockets onto it, looking around him as he did so, as if seeing this familiar decor for the first time. Then he would go over to the mirror and smooth his hair thoughtfully. And he would unbutton his shirt and stroke his chest with one hand idly. In the mornings I would run his bath and hold his cigarette for him so he could smoke it voluptuously while performing the ritual of soaping and rinsing. From time to time he would acknowledge my presence.

"All right?"

"All right."

Whereupon he'd nod, almost as a reflex action. He would often get up in the middle of the night for a drink of milk. Then he'd sit in the sitting-room and run a video cassette. He had a large collection of horror films, thrillers and epics, along with many blue movies which he often viewed. I'd hear him get up, invariably waking me from my nervous sleep. I'd wait a while before joining him on the settee. He'd sit up abruptly as if caught out: "I've woken you up again! Forgive me."

"It's all right," I'd lie, "I wasn't asleep."

He'd stare at my naked body and, smiling, fondle my cunt: "Why are you blonde down there as well?"

He never listened to my answer. Immediately we'd be absorbed again in the film – always silent, since he used to turn down the sound in order not to wake me.

Sometimes he wouldn't get back in the evening. I'd wait up a long time for him, nibbling at cold bits and pieces of food from the fridge, and usually curled up by the telephone. Around midnight he might call me:

"Everything all right? Yes? I'm on my way back …"

He'd find me in bed and would lie down very carefully beside me. I used to bury my head against his chest and smell the distinctive heavy scent I knew so well from our lovemaking. I'd feign sleep but his hand would truffle at my moist vulva and he would fuck me, usually imagining I was in fact fast asleep. On those occasions he was hard, selfish and implacable, yet I still experienced unparalleled pleasure since he would soon afterwards give me further proof of his desire.

On certain nights he drank more than usual, which was his excuse for playing out various fantasies he did not wish to admit to when sober. Once he made me lie nude on the floor, ordered me to stay absolutely still, and poured some red liquid over my neck. He then stood back and stared at me a long time. Another evening he made me kneel on the carpet.

"Lean forward."

I felt his breath on my neck. I bent over as far as possible, arms folded across my nape. He made me open my legs, grasped my buttocks tightly, and placed his mouth to my anus, his tongue moistening me there and giving me shivers and gooseflesh in the process.

"Don't move."

He penetrated me carefully and I found I was biting my lip throughout this long and slow advance, which indeed was probably if anything, too deliberate, too clumsy. I wanted to tell him that I consented, I was waiting for him, welcoming the inevitable pain. He slid forward into me while I drowned in blood-red, overwhelming waves. At last he stopped, only to begin moving slowly back and forth. The rhythm accelerated and I felt an intense almost liquid heat seep through me. His hand grasped my cunt then entered it, to rub that sensitive flesh separating us. He came silently, pulling out of me quickly – a loathsome sensation. I fled into the bathroom and washed away the shame of failure. It was the first time it had happened with him, and we had completely spoiled this incomparable communion. He often tried it again since then, but never managed to make me come that way.

One evening he didn't need Dutch courage: he was quite sober when announcing to me in a voice he thought was relaxed, "You know you really must find a flat ..."

I didn't reply. What could I have said? I know I flushed and my hands began to shake. He didn't want me any more. Full stop. Embarrassed by my silence, he went on: "She's going to come back."

I wanted to leave at once and rushed to the suitcase that was still standing against the wall. But he hurriedly stopped me.

"No Joy, not now. Stay tonight at least."

I cried and stayed. He made love to me particularly tenderly and cradled me to sleep with his mouth pressed against my hair, cuddling me in a way he'd never done before. I fell asleep telling myself that tomorrow he'd forget and I'd stay on. But next morning, just as he was leaving, he turned round and said to me:

"I'll be back for you at noon."

"Where will I go?" I sighed.

"I've found a friend who'll put you up for a few days."

I nodded, but swore to myself I'd leave and go somewhere he'd never find me. I shut the suitcase again, saying goodbye to the apartment in which I'd been so happy – the wardrobes, the bedroom with its unmade bed, the too-soft settee in the sitting-room, and the kitchen with its dripping tap. I neatly stashed my last hundred franc note in my purse and waited for him to come back and collect me.

The friend was called Holzer and lived on the Boulevard Port-Royal. His flat was antiquated and dismal, with a bedroom at the dark end whose walls were decorated with grey striped paper. The wooden bed faced the window, which overlooked the courtyard. Grubby grey curtains hung slightly crooked because many of their rings were missing.

"You'll be fine here, for the moment ..."

He kissed me.

"I'll leave you to get settled in, as I've an urgent appointment. I'll ring you in the afternoon and we can spend an evening together."

I clung to him, hit by sudden panic.

"When will you ring? You're sure you will? Don't leave me on my own ... Tonight?"

"As soon as I can."

"When, Marc? Tonight?"

"Not tonight, Joy. She's arriving soon."

I let him go. I unpacked my suitcase and hung my dresses in the wardrobe whose door creaked each time it was opened. I remembered my New York apartment, which now seemed positively palatial. Then I thought about Bruce and Joelle. I tried to recall the softness of her skin, her elusive and individual scent – everything she would be giving Marc in a few hours. Oddly enough, such thoughts did not upset me. I was too preoccupied to feel jealousy. I was scared, because this wretched grey room bore a horrible resemblance to the little rented room where I'd spent four years of waiting for mother to come back for me. It had that same carpet and that same wardrobe. No, I wasn't sad; I felt afraid.

Marc's friend was a nice, obliging and discreet guy. He called on me.

"Do you have everything you need? I hope everything will be OK. Come and have a look at the bathroom. And this is the kitchen here. Make yourself at home."

He smiled politely but distractedly.

"I forgot to introduce myself. Holzer. Jean-Claude."

He was rubbing his hands together in embarrassment.

"I almost forgot: it's annoying, but the telephone line's not quite long enough to stretch into your room. It goes as far as the middle of the corridor."

He began laughing and I joined in. I knew I'd be spending hours on the phone in the middle of the corridor.

I fell asleep on my unfamiliar bed, dreaming that I was arriving at the rail terminus of a distant capital. The place was all decked out with flags and banners and there was a welcome from a delirious crowd, while the man in my life appeared at the end of the platform. But the sun caught his sunglasses, and there was such a dazzling reflection that I could not be sure who he was ...

I woke furry-mouthed, my heart pounding, and had to drink some water from the tap since the refrigerator was empty. I rang Alain and his secretary informed me that he was away. I then addressed a little prayer to the God who watched over lost girls, begging Him to get me out of this grey prison double-quick, on the grounds that I hadn't deserved it as yet. I wandered around the funereal flat with its Louis XVI sitting-room, dirty furniture and threadbare carpets. It was all thoroughly bourgeois, a real dentist's waiting-room. China flower vases, pictures hanging askew – everything I loathed. I'd have loved to hide in one of Marc's wardrobes among his clothes and die there, suffocated by my memories.

I developed a headache, managed to find a couple of sleeping pills, and swallowed these with some lukewarm water. Then I curled up in bed and waited for a sleep which was prompt enough to catch me by surprise.

Next morning Jean-Claude woke me at nine, asking me if I'd like some coffee. I got up like a whirlwind, showered, pulled on sweater and jeans, and drank the scalding coffee, giving him a goodhumoured greeting.

"You're really attractive," he said gallantly. "A woman's beauty is best judged in the morning. And on that basis, you're even better looking after you've just got up."

"Maybe I do look nice in the morning," I said dreamily, "but I always get up late in the morning."

I rushed off, planting a kiss on his startled forehead. The morning was a very busy one for me: retrieving my other luggage and things from Avenue de Breteuil, and sending off a protest letter to Lausanne.

I'm out on the street, I don't have anywhere to go any more, and I've had to cadge a bed for the night. This is all your fault. It's all come about through your lack of interest. Why didn't you warn me, at least? Write, or ring me, but do something. I'm all on my own, mother. Do you realize this?

In the small red notebook where I've always listed the important occasions in my life, I had set down the fact that my happiness lasted ten days. Nine nights and ten days, to be exact, which seemed to me longer than an entire year. Ten little days, nothing special. A sad appraisal of Joy-my-loves, time lost, wrong turnings – to this grey room overlooking a courtyard. That long road leading to chilly solitude in a strange room. Yet thousands of hands would reach out towards me if I ventured out into the light of day! Why should I always be a voluntary recluse? Why and for whom?

CHAPTER THIRTEEN

Alain returned to Paris. As soon as I heard his voice I asked him for help: "It's Joy, I'm back."

"Where are you, though? I called your home and somebody answered me and said you didn't live there any more. Where are you?"

"I'll tell you about it. Oh Alain, please ask me to dinner tonight ..."

He hesitated a moment.

"Right you are, I'll ... What time suits you?"

"Any time," I laughed. "Any time at all. Whenever you want."

I laughed hysterically and then he was laughing too.

"Till tonight, Joy my love ..."

I felt immensely relieved. Alain would help me escape from my prison. He would set off to conquer the furthest planet if I asked him: he alone put me first, gave me the sort of priority afforded to war veterans and pregnant women on the Métro. I'd always have the right to a seat, next to him. Yet did I have the right to rely on him as friend or brother when his own feelings about me were very different? Alain desired me physically, of course, but that wasn't what held me back. The sexual relationship is inevitable between two people who love each other. With Alain, however, after the physical pleasure there remained love. And that I couldn't accept.

I left the telephone in the middle of the passage and returned to the grey room the sun never reached, especially not when it was fine outside.

Something important happened during the course of a summer I spent in the Dordogne. I had just turned eighteen and was all alone in the big house, waiting for mother's return from a trip to London. She would leave from time to time, for a week or two, saying she was on business. I never did know what business she meant. Anyway, during those memorable holidays I reigned over my court of admirers, who assiduously strove to satisfy my slightest whim. I liked to undermine their self-esteem and play on their vanity. I delighted in hurting those too vulnerable or too available, and I'd stir up jealousies, rivalries and intrigues. I was thoroughly odious, as nasty and foolish as one can be at eighteen if one has a high opinion of oneself but no understanding.

At the end of August, the time for thunderstorms and farewell parties, I was invited to a reception by some friends living nearby. Their remarkable house was in fact a castle built on a sheer rock, and bristled with turrets and crumbling battlements. I'd chosen the person who'd have the good fortune to accompany me to this party I recall with some nostalgia. My partner was to be a tall youth, fair and pale and smooth as a marble statue. He was extraordinarily graceful, almost androgynous, and there was something feminine about his walk and his rather high voice. Eric always kept out of my teasing games and blushed more than I ever did if there was boasting about relationships I'd had. He'd never utter the vulgar words we adored and which we used constantly. He seemed surprised I'd asked him to take me to the castle:

"I'm not the sort of fellow you're looking for, Joy. And you're not my ideal type, either. So what's the point of going together?"

I was mortified by his lack of enthusiasm. I'd never imagined that anyone could stand up to me. So I threatened and stamped my feet. I wanted him to accompany me and at last he gave in. In those days no one resisted me for long.

We spent a wonderful evening, with a very elegant crowd. The girls seemed to have been hand-picked for their looks and style, and were shown off to advantage by the innumerable candles lit throughout the enormous rooms. People even arrived from Paris during the course of the evening. Giggles and whispers swirled up the marble staircases towards the gilded ceilings. Gusts of heavy scent wafted through the greenhouse containing thousands of roses and orchids. Flickering flames from the candelabra were reflected in the gilt picture frames and the rich hangings. Jewels sparkled and chilled wine made eyes brighter still. It was lovelier than a dream.

That summer night's incomparable sweetness, the velvet suits and lace dresses, all evoked a bygone era. As I plunged into a whirlpool of music and laughter I half expected to meet at the start of a waltz the diaphanous silhouette of Yvonne de Galais on the arm of the tall Meaulnes.

Eric followed me around silently and whenever I was about to desert him temporarily, he would grasp my hand and say: "Don't go off and lose me. I don't know a soul here."

In a drawing-room dappled with violet light an attentive group of listeners surrounded a greyhaired man sitting in front of a pedestal table. We went over to them. The man bent over a pale girl's hand, which she held out, laughing. The faces clustered behind her looked like wax masks. Someone shouted for silence.

"Let him concentrate. Don't put him off!"

The girl holding out her hand had another bout of nervous laughter. The man looked her in the eye and told her drily:

"Don't laugh! I see dark clouds forming round you. The fire already burning, I can't do anything about it ..."

His face haggard, the stranger rose abruptly to his feet and pushed away the various hands extended towards him.

"No. I can't do any more. It's too hard."

He departed, while the young people thronged round the girl, who was staring at her palm as if hoping to decipher these dark predictions.

"Muriel, you're not scared are you? For God's sake, you don't believe all those horrible ..."

"No," Muriel replied rather shakily, "I'm not scared. I've never believed in that sort of nonsense."

I had a sudden brainwave. I turned to Eric, who couldn't conceal his concern.

"Wait for me here. I'll be back."

I ran down the long corridor leading to the garden. The greyhaired man was striding smartly towards the cluster of bushes by the main gate.

"Excuse me, Monsieur."

The man in black turned round. I caught sight of his worried face in the darkness.

"What do you want? I have to go, I'm late."

Holding out my hand I went up to him.

"*Please*, Monsieur, do tell me ..."

The man stared at me. His expression grew more relaxed and then he took hold of my hand in his own, which was cold. He spoke very hoarsely, deliberately.

"Your guiding light – because as you know, we are led by the light! – that light is favourable. But you must pay the price for your good fortune and long life. You'll waste your energy seeking one man, and this will be a mistake, for all men will love you. You are only on this earth in order to suffer and to love. You'll be in love once only and it will be too late, it's always too late. Delay is our curse, and the faster we go the further we fall behind."

I gazed at him in alarm. His eyes seemed to be blurred and anxious. He grasped my hand.

"People always ask me questions, but I don't know what the future brings. I'm not an initiate, I only receive premonitions. As for you, one day you'll set off on a terrifying journey, you'll be going to meet the unknown. And your life will begin again on that day ... Let me go now, I've told you the most important thing. I'm late."

He hurried off into the night without a second glance. I went back to the party, mixing with the carefree guests. I rejoined Eric after a while. He was waiting for me glumly.

"I need a drink," I told him.

He dashed off and found a bottle of champagne. He poured me a glass, and I drank the fizzing liquid at one gulp. Glass after glass, I then finished off the whole bottle without succeeding in slaking my desperate thirst. A silence seemed to have descended upon the yew trees and shrubs, and the lighthearted atmosphere had dissipated: there was now a curious tension among the various couples who seemed to be sobering up.

"Come on," Eric said. "You ought to go home, you'll be sick."

I found myself sitting in his car and then we were driving away into the night. I shut my eyes and must have passed out. But I had a rude awakening – shouts and screams. Eric had stopped the car on the roadside verge. Ahead of us a grim crowd of spectators watched a car blazing in a ditch. I got out like a robot. I knew what I would see – a contorted corpse, with a lace gown charred by flames. Before it was consumed, I noticed that Muriel's bleeding body extended one hand, open even in death. Since then, I've never forgotten the dull, listless look of the greyhaired man, and his words seem to beat inside my brain: the endless pursuit which is to exhaust me, the grim journey in search of the unknown ... My destiny is mapped out and I must follow its route, for I am powerless, condemned to go right to the very end.

I keep seeing certain scenes again, although time has begun to fade those unforgettable images – the greyhaired man's strange eyes and Muriel's body burning in the wrecked car. Why did I remember them on that particular evening? Alain's friendly and comforting presence made me forget my nightmares. He held me close to him and told me he'd thought he'd never see me again:

"You're here, Joy my love. You've come back."

He was nibbling my earlobes and I scarcely knew where I was, for I'd been deprived of tenderness for so long. I related my most recent news to him and he shook his head in astonishment.

"No, it's not possible ... But I'm here now, you know ... You'll have to come over to my house ..."

I knew he meant it, but his generosity concealed his passion. I could guess his depressing train of thought: *He's not the man for you, Joy, won't you realize that?* There was a hint of jealousy – or anger – in Alain's expression.

He suggested that I go and sleep at his place, which meant sleep with him and I refused. I'm not quite sure why I did. I still needed someone, anyone, to make love to me, to get me over Marc – but I shook my blonde locks.

"No, not tonight."

He reacted very well to this.

"Tomorrow, perhaps?"

"Tomorrow if you like."

He took me back to Boulevard Port-Royal and when I said goodbye I kissed him for a long time, on the lips, and it was all I could do not to invite him in. I waited until his tail-lights disappeared round the corner of Boulevard Saint-Michel before climbing the dusty staircase. The flat was dark and unfriendly. I walked down the long passageway, stumbling over the telephone. A strip of light under the door of the grey room warned me that there was someone there. I understood. Marc was lying on the bed, his shirt undone. When he saw me he sat up furiously.

"Where were you?"

His voice was hard, unpleasant and irritable.

"How dare you ask me that?" I retorted aggressively.

"My poor darling," he said, shaking his head, "you never understand anything."

He dragged me towards him, unbuttoning my dress. Then he pushed it up past my thighs, tugged down my panties and took me awkwardly against the wall, dry, tight and indifferent though I was. He delivered a series of cruel, violent and pointless thrusts.

"I need you, do you understand? I think about you all the time. And about fucking you too."

He let himself go, inundating my cunt. I remained unmoved and suspicious, but a spasm of heat surged through my loins as I felt him ejaculate inside me. I felt revived and triumphant, poor fool that I was. He jammed my mouth against his wet prick and I took it. My spittle mingled with seed and I felt the blood course once again through his warm shaft. I stopped and dared to confront him.

"I won't go all the way."

He was leaning against the wall.

"Shut up and make me come."

He was red and sweating, showing himself in his true colours

129

at last. He was the first to look away.

"I'm going to milk you, since that's what you're here for."

I gripped him very hard and jerked him in desperation, using abrupt strokes which made his cock throb in my hand. I felt his prick swell, then harden, the bluish veins stood out along the glistening skin as if about to burst, and then a white jet spattered my dress and bare legs, spilling tiny gouts of venom to poison my very soul.

I turned away from him, soiled, ashamed and nauseous. After some time he adjusted his clothing and grabbed my shoulder.

"Why do you behave like this? I leave her, *her*, in order to come and see you, and you don't even understand!"

I was just about to say that that wasn't enough for me, when I realized I was going to lie, because it was enough. I collapsed in his arms, trembling. In a moment of aberration I'd almost lost him.

"Forgive me, darling, but I'm not happy here, it's like a brothel ..."

"You're my little whore," he whispered, smiling.

Tears filled my eyes and I cried on his shoulder.

When he left he promised me he would not touch her that night.

"I swear to you I won't, Joy."

I thought it was a bit unfair, since she needed sex too. It wasn't her fault. He came back the next day, waking me at dawn. He lay on top of me and entered me without saying a single word. He made love to me wonderfully slowly. And that evening also he returned and we had dinner in a little place on the Boulevard Port-Royal. We then went back up into the grey room and he lay against me and fell asleep. Much later I woke him.

"Marc, it's very late. You must go. She's waiting for you."

"Yes, you're right," he said, nodding, as he looked at me gravely. "I should go."

He rang me several times during the days that followed.

"How's it going?"

"All right. I'm getting used to it. Are you coming over?"

130

"No, not tonight. Maybe we could take a trip somewhere..."

I agreed and hung up after my usual whispered endearments to him. I woke with a start, having fallen asleep on top of the bed. I must have been dreaming, for I had a clear picture of an Irish beach buffeted by stormy winds.

Mother called me from Lausanne.

"Hello, Joy my love – how awful, I forgot to warn you! Don't hold it against me, but I really didn't know you were coming back. And there you were with nowhere to go! I'm so embarrassed, Joy, but I couldn't do anything else – Albert went on so about it. He couldn't refuse his friends and besides it's important for business. Tell me, my poor darling, where's this place you're at now?"

I told her all about the grey room and the creaking wardrobe.

"Good heavens, how ghastly. And what about your work, Joy? Ah well, you can manage on your own I'm sure, after all you're grown up now."

I replied that she was quite right, of course, and hung up. This little set-up stung me into action. I got coffee for Jean-Claude, buttered a mountain of bread, made up, did my hair and put on some nice clothes. I felt hyper-active and full of confidence. I intended to organize my life, get going and be a success.

For a whole week I besieged the offices of photographers and agents and even of Goraguine, who gave me a cool reception. I paid Margo a surprise call and found her in bed with a lanky German girl with prominent tits.

"Darling you're crazy, it's still dark," she'd said yawning, when she opened the door.

I asked Alain to lend me two or three hundred francs for a few days.

"Of course, stupid."

I opened my window wide. Smells from the kitchen would drift up from the courtyard, but higher up I could see a patch of

131

blue sky between the rooftops and the crooked chimneys. I sorted through my things: my souvenirs of New York, books of matches from Steve's restaurant, the visiting card presented by Henri – he of the flight home, who was prepared to pay so handsomely for what had no price tag.

Unable to sleep, I spent whole nights tossing and turning in the wooden bed, constantly mulling over plans and fantasies for hours on end.

One night I got up in a state of desperation and had the urge to stroll through the deserted streets. Looking back, I know I was in fact seeking something which had obsessed me since one particular sexual encounter with Marc in that grey room so reminiscent of those anonymous Parisian *hôtels de passe* to which prostitutes took their short-time clients. My thoughts went back to Uncle Gaspard. I for one would never know the languid boredom of those long-defunct provincial brothels ...

I started walking along Boulevard Saint-Michel, waiting for the incident which would *inevitably* occur. Neon reflected off the wet pavements, while gusts of wind sprayed flurries of rain at me. A car drew up alongside. I kept walking, uneasy and tense, caught in that electric glare trying to disconcert me. I eventually turned my head, very slowly. A grey Citroen. The shape of someone leaning across the already lowered window.

"Good evening."

The voice was a little hesitant. I imperceptibly slowed down, telling myself I was crazy, completely demented and what was I doing anyhow. I'd get nowhere fast this way.

"Can I give you a lift anywhere?"

I looked at him again and moved nearer the kerb. He continued crawling along and smiled nervously at me.

"Getting in?"

I stopped and looked him full in the face. My heart beat so fast that my breasts must have been quivering.

"What do you want?" I said in a coarse, cynical tone I considered appropriate under the circumstances.

"How much?"

I winced.

"What is it you want?"

132

The deafening metallic din of a heavy lorry drowned the main part of his answer.

"... car ..."

I looked at him scornfully.

"Will a hundred francs do?"

I did not reply and began to walk off, shrugging.

"Hey, don't run away, tell me how much ..."

I gave him a sidelong look.

"Two hundred."

He braked sharply.

"Right. Get in!"

He opened the door and I got into the car, terrified. Once again I was afraid of not having the courage to go through with it to the bitter end. Reassured and triumphant, my client adopted a familiar tone.

"You're not annoyed are you ... Two hundred ... I mean at that price I assume you'll give me the full works?"

I lit a cigarette, shaking, and said:

"Shut up and get a move on, I'm in a hurry ..."

I showed him the way, telling him to stop the car under the very windows of the flat in which Marc had so hurt and angered me. The man pushed back his seat and began fumbling with his belt.

"The money first."

He found a bulging wallet and feverishly extracted a couple of hundred franc notes which he passed to me.

"Look, will you let me play with your tits?"

"That'll be a hundred extra."

He handed me another note nervously.

"Here, let's see them."

I opened my blouse and arched forward so that my generous breasts thrust almost into his face. He began fondling them with his sad, cold, loveless hands. He had clumsy, furtive hands which lacked any imagination, yet he liked what he was doing and uttered a series of groans.

"You have nice ones ... ah, what a fine pair of titties ..."

He freed himself and then proffered a bluish-looking prick.

"Here, take it."

I stroked it vigorously, detached enough to watch for any of the telltale signs, but the penis suddenly twitched without my feeling the least trace of any liquid spasm.

"Now," the man moaned.

I bent over him and proceeded to suck the erect, dead, anaesthetized object which seemed so devoid and deprived of any lust or vice and which must have known only greedy fingers and transitory mouths. I tried my best to feign passion and the man tensed, then started flailing his arms around, groaning.

"Whore, slut, you just love it, don't you? You're going to take it all, you're all the same, sluts and slags and whores ..."

I speeded up the rhythm of my movements and he suddenly pulled out of my mouth and gripped his cock in one hand. His eyes bulged from their sockets and he was foaming at the mouth.

"Take a look, you whore! Have a look at a man's spunk..."

I turned my head away in disgust but felt warm drops splash my wrist.

Soon afterwards, when he had recovered and done up his disordered clothes, he glaced at me in embarrassment.

"You're different, aren't you? You're not like the others. You even look nice after doing it."

I rushed off without a word, just a wave before I disappeared into the darkness. I remember his wounded, pathetic expression. He must have hoped I'd stay, for I heard him shout:

"Come back, won't you?"

I was racked with sobs. I was ashamed of myself and pitied him, even while cursing those emotions in me which had ruined this extreme test – for I had not seen it through to the end.

I was back in the grey room just as the sun was rising behind the crooked chimney stacks. I prayed for forgiveness, but had an uneasy premonition all the same. I found I was scurrying about aimlessly until I heard the phone ring as if to warn me that the danger came from there.

"Everything all right?"

It was Marc. He sounded uneasy.

"Yes, all right. Life's fine," I said, very apprehensively. "I've got a lot of plans. And I miss you, you know."

"I'm glad to hear you talk like that, Joy. I knew you understood, right?"

"Understood what?" I asked weakly.

"Things will be different between us from now on, but still fantastic ..."

"Marc, you're hiding something from me."

"I didn't want to tell you on the phone, but maybe it's better that way after all. Well, Joy – I'm getting married."

CHAPTER FOURTEEN

The most important part of a love story is the end. An hour too long, a day less, and everything is utterly changed. What remains is only padding, the detritus of passion, for like the rhythm of life itself the sentiments that attract, bind or separate two human beings are subject to birth, growth, ageing and inevitable destruction. After hearing that terrible announcement I remained numb. Ever since I'd known Marc I'd subconsciously dreaded a scene like that, relayed to me via the twisted cord of a telephone left in the middle of a corridor.

Just as a sentry on watch for the enemy during the night is terrified by the prospect of seeing him appear – and finally does catch sight of him – I too felt a sense of relief. As he loads, the sentry must surely experience a sort of calm, knowing the enemy is facing him, out there in the open. The will to survive sweeps aside fear. That wire reuniting me with Marc was too taut, it cut into my flesh too deeply for me to bear the pain for long.

I love Marc. Any successor to him will be only temporary and second best. Let no one ever tell me my love is irrational, excessive or futile. My love corresponds to my psychological needs, so Marc is vital to me. He is my victim because I was willing for him to disrupt my life. One never conquers fate.

Afterwards I cosseted myself for hours in the grey room, curled up on that bed without an eiderdown. Once again I flicked through those faded photographs in my mind: our meeting at the cemetery, the first time we made love, and the last. I sat in front of a mirror to see if I'd cry, but I wasn't crying. I told myself I was a fool, since it wasn't a parting as such and I'd go on seeing him as often as I wanted.

136

I gave way to a long period of aimless wandering and erratic behaviour. I'd upset and worry people by my sudden emotional outbursts of one sort or another. I developed bad habits too: I'd bite my nails and indulge in vile little fantasies like some frustrated nympho. And I got to know some new shopkeepers – at the wine store and the tobacconist's. Cigarettes and whisky. Female alcoholism, following upon heartbreak or sexual indiscretion, which are so often identical, usually begins with beer. At a friend's house or in a bar a request for beer is nothing unusual. Beer is associated with obesity rather than heavy drinking. I'd get drunk on beer, then bourbon, then both together. Hangovers are even less pleasant than disappointed loves. When night fell, I would return to the grey room carrying my tri-pack of Munich and I'd blithely sip my trio of lukewarm cans while eating an apple or some yoghourt, as though following a bona fide diet.

Once a week I used to have dinner with Alain, who was invariably gallant and nostalgic. I received discreet pressures from his huge male mitt on my small paw. He was putting up with the situation. He no longer suggested I should sleep at his place, but seemed eager to satisfy my every whim, sighing as if to say: "Ah, Joy, if you only would!"

I certainly would have liked to, in fact. My memories of him were reassuring and pleasant enough, yet I was deterred by the possible complications. Our relationship was too well established and our platonic little dinners too affectionate for us to destroy this nice balance through a few hours of abandon. I no longer felt capable of explaining and justifying my motives for doing particular things, and certainly reluctant to start each day that way. I was in a difficult, touchy state, living on the edge.

I was also indecisive and nervous. Often I did feel a vague desire for him, but through laziness, the bourgeois fear of complication, I would hold my tongue and pretend not to notice the burning looks focused upon me whenever I turned away for a moment. I might have given in, however, if he had taken the initiative and pulled my dress impatiently, saying: "Joke's over, Joy my love. I want to fuck you, relax a bit so I can undress you ..." God how awful. Alain would never behave like that. He'd have whispered: "Joy my love, forget your problems and depressions. Put your head on my shoulder, close your eyes and be happy!" His large, timid, hypocritical hand would have patted my neck, then brushed against my breasts or stomach, and liking that, I'd have said nothing. How many devastating passions, celebrated loves or extraordinary pleasures are stifled by timidity even before birth?

Marc always used to ring me at the same time, around six p.m. The hour when dog meets wolf, mother called it, and I believed her.

"Everything all right?"

I would describe my day and he'd say "That's good" or "That's not so good" – according to whether I'd worked or dawdled the time away in the grey room. He'd often repeat the same phrase: "I can't talk now," adding: "Eight o'clock, OK?" I never once told him it wasn't. And he always hung up complaining "Just a moment!"

Immediately I'd get ready. I wanted to look heartrendingly beautiful – sparkling eyes and voluptuous mouth, a touch of subtle scent on smooth inviting skin. I went through a satin underwear phase, a suspender belt era, a season of black tights and in warm weather I opted for nothing at all. Which indicates how time flew.

Our duel continued as soon as we were face to face. Marc would try desperately to make me forget Joelle. At that time they were already living together and as I knew only too well she was grabbing anyone and everything within sight and reach. Marc made out that he no longer had time to take life easy, that he worked nonstop and hardly had five minutes to call his own ... Poor chap, his life was becoming hellishly awkward but (thank you God) he had an oasis, a paradise, a little corner of Valhalla – me.

The remainder of the evening was taken up with waiting for whatever would happen. Tension, unease, impatience too. He knew when he entered the grey room that I'd undress him slowly, looking him boldly in the eye – exquisite revenge and brief domination. With me he'd be as inventive as anyone could be, trying to go beyond the very limits of pleasure itself, but I'd be more demanding and watchful than ever, very quick to show how sensitive I could get the moment he fell short of perfection. There was often a bitter scent about that grey room and I attributed it to the Turkish cigarettes I now habitually smoked after making love. He would leave just before dawn, as if daylight might reduce him to ashes – that vampire of my senses, doomed to the eternal curse of night! Or perhaps he was only an absurd Cinderella, I never knew.

The New Year went off like a damp squib. No wild parties saw it in: it meant floods of tears and much angst for me, but the black depressive clouds did at last part to let the sun shine through. A laconic telex had reminded Alexander Goraguine of my existence.

My American B movie was breaking box office records. Audiences were apparently raving over my suntanned bottom ('new erotic French style'), the dollars were pouring in, and the other side of the ocean there were men sitting in the dark, overcome by my aggressive image magnified a thousand times on their screens, those mirrors full of fantasies.

The interrupted carousel began to revolve again, creakily. The anxiety makers and dream merchants reappeared. The phone was once again overloaded with scores of calls from jealous and opportunist good Samaritans. Friends multiplied. I remained aloof and detached. I amused myself considerably by monitoring the successive stages of Marc's jealousy: he could not abide the interest being taken in me, and I understood that he was scared of losing me. And little Joy knew quite well that her availability, her passion which had stood the test of time, and her sheer physical generosity made her unique and irreplaceable. He, the male, replete and sated with pleasure, was taking a poor view of that cage door now opening – behind which I had previously let myself be imprisoned. The defeat he was experiencing manifested itself in the neglect of various business deals he was on the verge of clinching. Marc had lost his proud image. No longer the arrogant conqueror with the golden touch, he clung despondently to his shattered illusions, hanging on to our complicity with visible distress.

I applied myself to the task of increasing his anxiety. I became maternal and sympathetic. That was the era of intimate little dinners slowly simmered on Jean-Claude's cooker, and of candles wavering on the rickety table of the grey room. I would spring surprises; tiny presents gift-wrapped in silk ribbons, and sudden spontaneous cuddles.

"I'm here, Marc. Shut your eyes."

Even through his closed eyelids I seemed to detect a baleful flicker of distrust. Suspicion blinded him and seemed to erode his tranquillity. However, I never did feel that pity he so dreaded. Having been reduced by circumstances to the level of an average man like any other, he came to resemble those others. Ordinary, limited, cowardly he might have been, but he *was* approachable, and I loved him for it, perhaps even more than when he had seemed so romantic.

One day I folded my new dresses inside out, rearranged my photos, and packed my bags. Then I wrote to Jean-Claude a note in pink marker-pen and for the last time in my life shut the door of the grey room.

With my own money I rented a large white studio flat on the top floor of a new block. Up there the sun shone all day long. The place was light and airy and from my end of the roof I could breathe the breeze coming in from the sea. I was dazzled by the white walls and sniffed at the new odours like an animal in its lair. I had only a bed, a pair of sheets, a blanket, a casserole, a frying pan and a bath towel, but I was free and easy. Marc came to see me every day but he didn't feel at all comfortable.

"I don't like Boulevard Exelmans."

"We'll move later, my love, when we're living together."

"I dislike concrete tower blocks."

"I'll build you a granite castle in the heart of Brittany and we'll hide there, some day."

He would have liked to admit that he missed the grey room, my unhappiness and that very fear which had made me depend on him. My independence thwarted him and my successes undermined his own self-confidence. I was affected by his moods, his hesitations and his sudden outbursts of love without hope or rancour. Marc was afraid of losing me, but nothing would have persuaded him to alter his way of life in order to keep me. Our meetings might be tinged with boredom and pleasant habit might sometimes blunt the edge of pleasure, yet the chains binding us daily bit deeply into our flesh. I tried hard to sustain that mental abstinence I'd initiated since the start of my stay in the grey room. I suppressed my more lecherous imaginings – those outrageous fantasies I indulged in my solitude. Saving myself for lovemaking, I resisted the temptation to masturbate. I was becoming a virgin again.

I was booked by a Bavarian production company for a fairly innocuous minor role in a boring, slowpaced six-hour TV serial. The PR man who was fairhaired and shy, harboured a platonic passion for me. He saw to it that I came over as the real star of the saga, a fact which visibly annoyed the prejudiced German actors.

A dinner in a fashionable restaurant had been arranged to celebrate the end of the shooting. Ten of us formed a rowdy bunch and, of course, when we entered this classy dive and sat down at the long table reserved for us, I caught sight of Marc and Joelle seated at a table nearby. That evening she was so beautiful that I was beset more by nostalgic memories than by jealousy. They seemed ill at ease, so different from how they were that night when I'd first seen them together, in a place so reminiscent of this, in the same area of town and at the very same hour.

Joelle smiled, gazing at me for quite a while, coolly yet tenderly too, before she got up and came over to give me a kiss. Her mouth brushed my cheek and I inhaled her subtle scent which I knew so well and had not forgotten. We clasped hands and I felt close to tears. She went back to sit beside him and both of them were looking at me, separately, throughout the meal, until a boisterous family group sat between us, masking me from them. When this disruptive gang finally left, the table opposite was vacant, and on it lay an empty cigarette packet and a napkin stained with bright red lipstick.

Marc rejoined me much later, his face haggard, and made love to me enthusiastically before he had to set off again as usual. It was five a.m. and Paris was just waking up.

He gave me a Cartier bracelet for my birthday – the kind you wear till your dying day. And we never ventured outside all day. Mother rang me at midnight: "Joy my love, it's your birthday. Lots of love and kisses, darling. I've bought you a *lovely* present. I'll give it to you in Paris when I come and see you ..."

I answered with a not very festive "Yes, right."

"What's the matter with you, Joy? I saw your recent photos and you looked marvellous ... I'm really proud of you, you know. I tell everyone that you're my daughter. Hello, Joy, Albert sends you a kiss, hello Joy I can't hear you ..."

I posed nude for *Lui*. Maybe I needed to show myself off to everyone, to be admired and arouse desire, just one more time. I imagined some lonely man drooling over my nakedness, my ripe breasts and blonde bush. No one ever understands that. Exhibitionist urges are somehow pathetic, especially when one is young and beautiful and everyone tells you so. As a result of this spread, numerous strangers got hold of my telephone number and rang me day and night asking me my price and availability. I felt acutely distressed, and even sick with myself for not having the courage to take up a challenge.

At about six one evening Marc returned from a trip, just as I was chatting on the phone to Margo. He rang twice, a long and a short ring, as he usually did, and I let him in. He was holding a copy of *Lui*. He flung me on the bed and slapped me. It didn't hurt. I felt no shame or anger, just surprise. I saw in his eyes that he regretted his action. He was assessing his error. I kissed him casually and as my hand went to my burning cheek, asked: "How are things?"

142

CHAPTER FIFTEEN

To believe one can retrace one's steps is invariably mistaken.
Once the caravan has set off, nothing can stop it, and whoever
turns for a backward glance is turned to a pillar of salt. I regret
nothing. My story is banal. I wanted to tell it because it is also
timeless. I wished to pay homage to the love which inspired me.
I ascended a steep hill from which I could discern all the
highways and byways of passion. I chose the most inviting
route, but it led nowhere. The days which passed no longer
held any surprises for me.

I expect everything and yet I suffer nothing, since the
decision to refuse or withdraw is mine alone. I accept the best
and the worst. The good and the bad. True and false.
Happiness and misery. Love and desire. They all form part of a
whole and it is futile to try to separate them, for when you grasp
the one you also necessarily lay hands on the other. I have at my
disposal the super-human strength which beauty gives; I distil
my youth carefully; I fill my head with fabulous memories
which will stay with me to the end.

I had a date with Marc at eight o'clock. He had rung me in the
afternoon to let me know he was free and had decided to see me.

"If you've arranged anything, just cancel it."

I duly cancelled an appointment. I fight using my own
weapons, which are availability and the particular fantasy I
alone can weave. Marc is in my power. I drag him towards our
mutual downfall. It's not possible to turn back. The road leads
to a horizon I alone know.

He rang my doorbell. One long ring, one short. I never gave
him a set of keys to the studio and he never dared ask. He looked
elegant in his beige cashmere sweater and blue shirt.

"I like you and I love you," I said.

I clung round his neck, intoxicated by the scent of verbena he exuded like an unlucky charm. As we were about to go out, our eyes met. I had put on for him my black net dress which emphasized my breasts. He hesitated. I knew by now the words to make him react.

"What are you afraid of?"

In the lift he tugged my dress above my waist so he could see my bare stomach and the pubic hair I had shaved and trimmed in the shape of a heart.

"Turn round."

I turned and he started stroking the blonde down and the wisps of hair visible between my buttocks. I've often looked at these myself in the mirror, craning my neck to do so.

I slipped into the double-parked car. The leather of the seats was cold and made me shiver. He had booked a table in a rather dull restaurant. He consulted the menu and ordered without asking me what I wanted, choosing the wines with the assurance of those who are never mistaken.

"I'd like you to take me back to your house," I murmured to him at one point.

I'd fantasized about seeing him in our Dordogne orchard, his white shirt open and his thin trousers stained with grass at the knees.

"The house won't let you share," I resumed, ill at ease.

The white wine was sharpening my tongue and clouding my mind. I slid a hand under the tablecloth in order to caress his thigh. He looked astonished.

"Not now."

Afterwards the car was gliding along a deserted boulevard, its wipers clicking monotonously at the rivulets of rain which distorted the glowing lights. By the liquid red haze of a halt sign, I saw him unbuckle his trouser belt. I leaned over to the talisman which quivered at each movement of my lips. He raised his haunches to thrust it deeper into my mouth and I found myself gagging with a keen thrill of pleasure.

"Stop."

I sat up slowly, my mouth moist, while he drove between two

144

cruising taxis.

"Where are we going?" I asked him with a sudden anxiety.

He stroked my parted thighs, although I hadn't really wanted him to. He turned left on to Boulevard Lannes and stopped in the darkness further on, by the sparse bushes of a dusty square. He pushed back his seat, switched off the lights and opened one window.

"Go on now."

I looked proudly at him and bent over him once again. I wanted to give him pleasure. I had to be violent, agonizing. I shut my eyes. I liked sucking him off. I fell upon him like a lovesick bitch.

"Ah," he sighed, "that's it!"

I opened my eyes and noticed that the interior light was on. Slowly I took the prick out of my mouth, and another sort of electric current coursed right through me. Various dark outlines were pressing against the glass, all around the car. My eyes were blurred with tears, as I'd almost been choking, but I realized belatedly that the ghostly shapes were making the same motions – regular, rhythmic and obvious. These faceless men were masturbating while they watched me. When they saw my startled face, they crowded round the vehicle. They began to sway, caught up in a press of bodies, voyeurs pitching and tossing, rocking back and forth, rubbing themselves against the windows. Marc had flung his head backward and was holding his prick, lit now by the instrument panel.

"Go on," he groaned. "Finish me off."

His forehead was soaked in sweat and his mouth quivering. I wanted to whisper words of love but dared not and slowly swallowed his prick once more, very conscious of the anonymous stares following every movement of my neck as I rocked to and fro. Beams of light illuminated my lips. The peeping toms were armed with torches, which they had artfully taped up so that only a pencil-thin strip of light, precise as a laser, would pierce the darkness to reveal the exact and essential spot on which their sinister pleasure was focused. The unseen spectators shone their beams on my distorted mouth. Some of them were scratching against the car doors like frightful animals. I accelerated my rhythm. Marc tensed still more.

"Yes, Joy, yes."

He pressed the button controlling the electric window, and cold air hit my face. Terrified, I realized that the window was now fully open and shaking hands were grabbing at my breasts just as Marc was coming into my burning mouth. Surprised by the copious flood of liquid, I involuntarily jerked backwards towards the shadowy figures swarming round the windscreen, and thick warm gouts of sperm spurted over my dress. A hand burst through from the darkness to grope at my thigh. I tried to force it away, but then my hand was suddenly grabbed and tugged out of the window. I could feel various scarcely visible but hugely distended pricks shooting off all over my fingers. Marc brutally hoisted up my dress, shouting:

"Take a look at the most beautiful girl in the world!"

The shadow men pressed against the door as if they wanted to crush the car to pulp, and their torches played over my soiled dress and my bare, glistening thighs. One voyeur managed to plaster himself against the window, thrusting his erect sex inside at me. Marc pushed me forward by the nape of the neck, whispering: "Take him in your mouth, go on, do it for me."

I broke away in horror and began screaming. My screams startled the shadows, and they disappeared in a flash. Only one man remained. He was tall and hunched up and was calmly jerking himself off, spilling his milky smears across the windscreen. Then Marc started the car suddenly, and it too jerked forward. There was a squeal of tyres as we drove off.

My heart beat so fast it was almost painful. I felt drunk and sick, hemmed in by that phallic forest born of the night. A tense silence hung between us, each waiting for the other to be the first to speak. I wanted him to justify his attitude, and doubtless he was hoping I would do the same. Beyond the silence a wall of secrets and memories was rapidly rising which separated us irrevocably from those who could never understand that energy fuelling our passions and obsessions. In the end it would part us too, when we had reached the point of no return. I had often been afraid of reaching the limit of our potential and of unwittingly crossing those last few feet separating us from the abyss.

I took his hand and kissed it tenderly.

"One must go all the way, don't you think?"

One evening I had asked the first lover who gave me an orgasm if he would show me everything, because I was ready for anything. "Surprise me, Benoit," I'd said to him.

"We haven't the time," he had replied. "Others will complete what I've begun."

He had been perverse and forceful, and right too – as far as he'd taken me. We hadn't even gone a quarter of the way together, for the heart tires sooner than the mind.

An icy breeze rushed through the car as it roared through the night at top speed. I was drunk with wind, and my hair whipped at my face.

"Where are you taking me?" I asked.

He did not reply and I dreamed that he was taking me to the ends of the earth, somewhere far away and outside ourselves. He stopped at Ville d'Avray, outside a closed service station. The ends of the earth are not as far as one imagines. An electrically operated metal shutter opened, revealing a man who nodded at us: "Good evening, Madame, Monsieur Marc."

We entered a bar full of smoke and music. Men and women were talking in front of the counter, and the place had the relaxed atmosphere of a provincial brasserie, all discreet laughter and the clink of glasses.

Marc steered me to the far end of the room, where faces peered from the shadow, looking at me with undisguised curiosity. A loud voice behind me remarked: "She's new, I've never seen her before." Hands seemed to brush my legs and breasts. Marc ordered drinks and the barman passed him a bottle of bourbon, giving him a conspiratorial and admiring wink. Pasted on the bottle there was a label which read *Monsieur Marc*. I drank the iced liquid and it soothed the irritation in my longsuffering throat.

"This is the temple of women. Men are only admitted in order to fulfil your fantasies. You can do whatever you like.

147

Take advantage of that."

A slender Brazilian woman passed in front of us, flashing a provocative smile at me. She was wearing a man's shirt, visible under it a white suspender belt which emphasized the dark tufted triangle of her sex. Two men appeared from the shadows and followed her into the dark recesses of the inner room. There was a general movement in that direction.

"Come and see," Marc whispered, pulling me along with him.

We went past a screen and through to a dark room. The Brazilian stretched herself out slowly upon a table placed in the centre of the room, where she was surrounded at once by about twenty spectators, mostly men, with a few attractive young women among them. The Brazilian was talking to a white-haired man.

The latter was stroking her long black hair and assisting her to install herself comfortably. When she was lying down, he kissed her on the lips and gently parted her lithe brown legs. Hands swarmed all over her prone body, unbuttoning her shirt, palping and kneading the voluminous breasts, whose brown nipples were now turgid. A man then extracted his penis from his trousers and moved into position facing the female organs on offer. The Brazilian spread herself still wider with her slim fingers. She was staring intently at the white-haired man who was stroking her cheek to reassure her. The man penetrated her roughly and she gasped.

There was some agitation among the circle of spectators and I saw men pulling out their pricks in order to rub them against her horizontal body. The man fucking her was tall and unattractive, his movements were regular, his style mechanical and his roughness calculated. He was systematically and without passion performing the act of possession, making sure of inducing an orgasm. The Brazilian shook her head from side to side, shut her eyes and passed one hand over her dry mouth. As she did so, she grasped a member being flourished at her and began jerking it violently. Then she opened her eyes again, rolling them frantically as she watched the silent crowd observing the inexorable onset of her paroxysm. A man bent over her and succeeded in inserting his prick in her mouth. She

148

engulfed it enthusiastically and I saw her cheeks bulge then hollow. With both her hands she squeezed the base of the man's tool, which turned beet-red. The man fucking her gradually slowed his rhythm. The whitehaired man was quietly masturbating under his folded jacket. Teasing hands worked at her nipples, while with a hoarse moan a man splashed her brown thighs. The man churning in her mouth pulled out and his seed dribbled down her lips.

The ceremony was unfolding in nerve-wracking silence punctuated only by heavy breathing, and by the moist slithers and suctions of kisses and embraces. The figures crouched around the table were faceless, anonymous. Everything had been reduced to a level of sexes, half-open clothes, pale patches of flesh and hands in motion, the whiteness of women's thighs. The absorbed faces might as well have been invisible. Ugliness no longer had any meaning. The man fucking the Brazilian sank inside to the very hilt, pulling her upwards to meet his thrusts as if trying to skewer her to the table. She raised her head to see her assailant finally withdraw. He was immediately replaced by a new intruder whose member was thicker still. Marc was standing behind me and at that moment he fumbled under my dress to see whether I was excited. When I felt his hand working its way into me I squatted slightly, lowering my haunches so that he could go even deeper. He removed his fingers, which, as they slid out, left a damp trail of moisture along my thighs.

"Wait a little longer," he told me.

My temples were clamped in a vice, my eyes smarted and I was intoxicated by the heavy odour of the entwined bodies. I felt an overpowering need to be handled and touched, a basic childish urge, and I knew Marc would refuse to assuage it, forcing me to see things through to the very end. Once again I found myself in the throes of the constant struggle which was tearing me apart.

On the table meanwhile, the Brazilian woman was shrieking every time an inexorable thrust pinned her back. Her hands flailed at the figures leaning over her. Some of the women were biting and gnawing at their hands, envying her her admirable pleasure. A pale young blonde whispered in my ear:

"She's about to come *again* ..."

I turned quickly to Marc.

"That's enough. I want to go now. I can't stand any more of this."

Marc looked at me contemptuously.

"You'll stay. I want to see you get fucked by these guys, understand?"

I let go of him abruptly, and headed for the exit, avoiding various groping and wheedling hands. I kept bumping into tightly glued bodies, brushing against naked flesh which my cigarette lighter momentarily illuminated. I reached a low dais surrounded by a fascinated crowd. A blonde was leaning with her palms against the gilded cornice that projected round the walls. Her convulsive movements made her thin body jut out, flaunting her black leather harness studded with nails. Round her neck was a collar, connected by a silver chain to a wide belt. From this belt hung more chains joined by metal buckles to her labia. A silver safety-pin ran through each nipple. Behind her a man crouched, buggering her slowly. She was turning her head from left to right and moaning. Her eyes had dark mauve shadows round them and her forehead was drenched in perspiration. Her face was twisted in a grimace and she uttered a cry which prompted shudders from the spectators. This unbearable cry was the expression of an unspeakable happiness. A man moved forward, grasped her hair and forced her to give him her mouth. He had filled her throat and tears were trickling down the chained girl's cheeks. Her cries were stifled now by the hard flesh wedged between her lips. A man stood beside her ensuring she came to no harm. With a pleasant smile he commented:

"Careful please, you can see she has pins in her breasts. Don't pull in the rings, she's been infibulated ..."

The sodomite withdrew, spreading the mutilated body wider to expose to the voyeurs the obscene and gaping orifice he had just abandoned. I was stunned. I had never imagined that orgasmic pleasure could become so pathetic. I was indifferent to the hands groping under my dress and fondling

150

my cunt. The spectacle of this abused, triumphant girl anni-
hilated my willpower. I'd never seen anything like it before.
I thought I could know and experience everything, but I
hadn't even gone halfway along the road to ultimate sexuality.
I was just a child, a vain bourgeoise lacking imagination,
Alice in the wonderland of perversion. I was discovering with
awe the deeper motivations of that vice which actually
reflects an incomparable beauty. I would have liked to go over
to the chained girl, kiss her parched lips, caress her swollen body
and tell her: "I desire you." Thanks to her I might come
to understand Pleasure, which only attains sublimity when
it is purged of all neurosis, all aesthetic constraints, all
demonstration of will, shame, or morality. I now knew I'd
never understand it – I who need to hold a man in my arms
before he takes me, I who like tender words and soothing
caresses, and promises never to be kept, and lying words in
blue ink on crumpled white paper. My sexual freedom is
conditional, supervised, hypocritical, endlessly challenged. I
am ordinary, just like most people. I have a heart.

Marc unbuttoned my dress, which fell to the floor like a
shroud. Shadowy figures flung themselves on me. Sticky
hands slid over my skin. Marc made me kneel and I was
encircled by a mass of distended pricks stiff and menacing. I
temporarily lost consciousness. Gross, quivering insects
fluttered and pecked and rubbed against my face, found my
mouth, caught in my hair, beat at my temples and slithered
over my neck. I endured an onslaught of pungent odours and
was slapped by tuberous objects being jerked by manic hands.
A red spotlight danced in front of my eyes. Marc was smiling
and twisting my hair, as one tugs a mare's mane to make her
raise her head. They came all over me, gradually covering me
in jissom, fleck by fleck, gout upon gout, a veritable snow-
storm. I was struck dumb, soaked, completely shattered. The
dark figures moved off stealthily and left me there on my knees
in the middle of the deserted room. Marc grasped my shoulders.

"Joy, you're all right, aren't you? Everything all right?"

He led me away to a white room where he cleaned me up. I
had been to hell or paradise, I shall never know which.

CHAPTER SIXTEEN

During the course of that long night of dementia when he let me glimpse some dizzying abysses, Marc had turned up the hourglass. In that dark drinking club somehow time had been interrupted, as when a film ends on a frozen frame, abruptly, and without the words THE END. The shock I experienced had wrecked the comparatively balanced life-style I'd managed to evolve. The schizoid quality my life had once had, now returned. My mind seemed to go round in circles, obsessed by a hedonistic morality which had hitherto never bothered me. Conflicting urges drove me to tie the leather lead around my neck and to crane forward hopefully for Marc's studded fist, but immediately I felt passive and fell into my depressive cycle I would indignantly, maniacally, repress this inevitable conclusion. I would contest the evidence, while doubt gnawed like an acid within me. I knew I'd lose Marc by remaining available and would win him for ever if I left. The appalling conviction haunted me that on that fatal night I had reached the acme of pleasure and the apogee of a lost love.

In challenge after challenge, we had gone beyond the limit, and Marc had quite consciously pinned me with my back to the wall of a dead end. I did not want to experience decline, deterioration and that slow death lying in wait together with the passage of time. And although I felt the desire to do so, I was afraid to rediscover the glowing depths of that hell, for fear of it seeming even less abnormal to me than I remembered.

Since that crucial night I lived a sort of double life. I would walk alongside myself, an unbearable and depressing case of split personality. I took refuge in an expiatory solitude. Marc no longer contacted me. He knew he had lost me by proving to me that my love was a shelter in which I curled up in order to escape my fantasies.

I could no longer ignore the conclusion. Anyhow, I decided to go on a sort of pilgrimage, back to the landmarks of my childhood. A night train took me to our house, which stood on a loop of the Dordogne. The grounds had been maintained as if I had left only the night before. My footsteps echoed on the flagstones. I found the books I used to read in one corner of the high chimney place. There was an old magazine folded into four, dating from five years ago, and playing cards in a pile, with the yellowed scrap of paper upon which were written the scores of that final hand. In my bedroom the copper bedstead gleamed in the half-light and when I opened the shutters, making them crack against the stonework, I realized that things, like people, continue to live on in one's absence. The process of ageing is inexorable, changing interiors and altering appearances.

I imagined Marc would give Joelle a child and that he would thus remove the last splinter embedded in my heart. Secretly I shall keep the priceless presents he unwittingly gave me, and which no one can ever take from me. The streets we crossed hand in hand. The cinema where I slept, head resting on his shoulder. The shop where he bought me a gold-plated heart. The hallway of a block of flats in which we sheltered from the rain. The café-tabac where he bought my cigarettes. The bakery where I used to buy warm croissants for breakfast, and all the other places which saw us living together – all these belong to me from now on. I could never see them again without thinking of him, and I am the richer for it. Those places carry associations, so I have the intuition that one day we will see each other again there: we may have a wrinkle or two more, the first grey hairs may show at our temples, but we'll be the same.

My life organized itself. It was shared between work which didn't interest me and people I didn't care about. On several occasions I did go round to Alain's to have him make love to me in his usual style, forcefully and insatiably. From time to time I'd drop in on Margo during my solitary rambles. Otherwise it was strangers who seemed curious to make my acquaintance. One day I learned that Marc had left Paris for good. I'd hoped for a letter, or a phone call at the crack of dawn one grey day ... A few months later Alain told me he was off on his travels to help set up a group of stores internationally. Bruce rang me several times from New York. His soft voice perturbed me. I realized he'd never kissed me or even touched me.

I don't need insignificant people.

I did feel I should set things in order. I remembered how my grandmother, whom I never knew well, was always tidying the mysterious contents of a little cowhide suitcase she had. In it were strange packets wrapped in tissue paper, a green leather wallet, a shell necklace, and a tiny engraved copper box from which there emanated – the only time I opened it – a faint scent of orange-blossom. I liked to surprise her in her bedroom, whose shutters were always half-open, winter or summer. The sun seemed loath to fade that hunched old lady still more, as she sat in her armchair dusting herself with a swansdown powderpuff. She would peer at me over her glasses, mischief sparkling in her blue eyes. Raising a finger, she'd say in a mysterious tone of voice that set me dreaming:

"You must always keep your memories tidy, Joy. Remember that ..."

One July morning I went to see her, bringing with me a bunch of poppies picked very early from the huge field that sloped down towards the village. I found her sitting in her armchair, facing the precious case, her eyes closed. For a long time I stayed there watching her sleep. I knew she had dropped off to sleep contentedly, for she was still clutching the green leather wallet.

Ever since then I've always sorted through memories and set them in order. I've written this book partly in the hope that one day it will become as important to me as that magic wallet was to her. Every night as I sat at the round table by the window, letting pen scratch over paper, I was putting things

154

in order.

Rereading these pages I find that what I've written rarely conveys the true flavour of my thoughts. At certain moments words slip away from me like landscapes glimpsed from a train. If when faced with the blank page objectivity is a proof of strength, I have failed in that. People, feelings and incidents appear in a context one tries to explain, for one always wants to explain it all in a book, but with hindsight it is all too easy to analyse whatever one did not understand at the time.

It happened one evening long after I'd given up expecting anything like that to happen. A yellow envelope in the letter box: the message I'd been awaiting so long, the supreme test, the confrontation with destiny. This envelope had been inevitable, as death will be one day. I inspected it gravely, feeling considerable anxiety. I was going to be born again. My disappearance wouldn't distress anyone. I'd soon be replaced and those who'd loved me would never suspect I'd simply answered a summons like this. The envelope contained only an airline ticket, a paper rectangle dancing in front of my eyes. A one-way ticket. Departure Orly-Sud, 08.20. Destination: Wellington. Hour of arrival: illegible.

I almost fell on my knees, clutching the ticket. I wanted to thank that God I too often forgot about. Somehow I knew that this was preordained to happen one day. I rushed to my dictionary. New Zealand, my God. North Island 143,000 pop. How small it was! Port on the Cook Straits ...

I imagined a sundrenched port with palm trees waving in the sea breeze and tattered children begging from the wealthy passengers disembarking from a transatlantic liner. Feverishly I turned the pages of the encyclopaedia which had never before seen such zeal. Zama, Zenobia ... ah Zealand see New ... New Zealand: 'group of two large islands of Oceania ... North Island ... volcanoes, geysers ...' I closed the book with a sigh.

I was bound for a land of volcanoes. I looked nervously at the ticket again.

Unlikely though it may seem, I had not yet asked myself the vital question: who had sent me the ticket? I kept turning it over and over in my hands, looking for the slightest hint. It was simply an airline ticket to New Zealand just like any other. There were only three people who would have invited me to a land of volcanoes. Alain, Bruce and Marc. Only three people who knew me well enough to assume I would actually set off towards the unknown. Marc, Alain, and Bruce. Only three men could make me cross the earth for them. Bruce, Marc, and Alain.

I tried to cheat, by ringing Alain's office. His secretary was away and no one seemed to know where he himself was. I was told politely that he had left instructions ... I rang Marc's home: someone would surely know where to find him. I heard the disconnected tone, and enquiries revealed that there was now no subscriber for the number listed ...

I rang New York. Bruce was on a business trip and would not be back for a month. Feeling thoroughly thwarted and helpless, I told myself I just couldn't leave France, abandon my country and way of life in order to go and meet someone I didn't know on a volcano-ridden island at the ends of the earth. All the same, I had to know whom I would be meeting out there. I wasn't *that* crazy. I wasn't *that* confused, nor was I lonely. No, I wasn't going to give in yet.

CHAPTER SEVENTEEN

My last suitcase was packed and I was sitting on top of it. It was bulging with secrets and useless souvenirs. The telephone rang. It was Margo, shouting: "You're mad, Joy my love. You're making a big mistake. They'll never let you get away with it, you can't just drop everything, work and all, and go off like this ..."

I replied that I had to go, it was written. I couldn't fight fate. Then the callbox pips and went and condemned me without reprieve.

I stowed my ticket for the volcanoes at the bottom of my bag, in the little pocket where I kept Uncle Gaspard's key. What advice would the old boy have given me, I wonder? Anyhow, I wrote mother a letter, for I was afraid of talking to her on the phone in case she persuaded me to change my mind. I knew I was going too fast, taking a big chance by not even trying to find out what I was letting myself in for, but it was just too bad. I wanted to see the volcanoes, the palm trees and the surf crashing against the sea-wall as it did at Crotoy, where mother used to take me during the winter to put colour in my cheeks. I demand tolerance, claim the right to make mistakes. And anyway, perhaps the domestic life – with children, evenings by the fireside and all that – awaited me only in Wellington, NZ. To the very last minute I kept listening for the phone and the doorbell. Maybe there'd be a carrier pigeon, some word or other to reassure me or give me the key to the enigma.

It was time. I closed up the flat and shut the front door. In the shuddering lift I swore I'd return. I passed the letterbox which would fill with letters I'd never open. What if Marc had written one of his "Joy my love" missives? So much the worse for him, it was too late, since I no longer even belonged to myself. My taxi splashed through the deserted streets and all the lights were on green, as if no one wanted to hold me back. Passers-by didn't give us a second glance: indifference aids important decisions. No tailbacks, no motorway accidents, no CRS to stop the taxi and ask for my papers. Nothing to stop me leaving.

Orly Airport, a bitter dawn. The driver hauled my luggage on to the pavement and asked me in a thick Provençal accent:

"You must have put everything but the kitchen sink in here. Why's it so heavy?"

I looked at him a little tearfully. His accent had really upset me, and sniffled:

"I *have* put everything inside."

A blue-clad stewardess guided me into the ghastly mist of the airport. I'd packed my glasses at the bottom of a suitcase and was thus virtually helpless, I couldn't see a thing. I was scared. By the embarkation gate I recoiled, after second thoughts about the volcanoes, and stopped in my tracks.

An authoritative voice was addressing me:

"Your luggage is registered. Kindly take your embarkation card."

I clutched on to the official.

"I don't want to go."

She stared at me with that lofty contempt reserved for invalids and the elderly should they happen to hold up the queue.

"I beg your pardon?"

"I no longer want to leave, it's all a mistake, I want to go somewhere else."

The air hostess looked at me slowly and suspiciously. Then, still staring hard at me, she shook her head.

"I'm sorry, but it's too late. Your luggage is already aboard the aircraft."

I stifled my sobs with my sleeve and walked on into the depths of the covered walkway. Welcome on board. A uniformed man showed me to a seat. I sat down. I no longer wanted to leave: perhaps I was mad, but I wanted to stay in Paris.

"I have to get off," I mumbled not very convincingly to the steward, "I've forgotten something …"

The steward brushed against my forehead as he leaned over.

"Too late, Mademoiselle, we're taking off."

Joy my love, you can't fight volcanoes. You might be going to your death, but you always knew it had to be. It was written.

I bought cigarettes and chewing gum, gilt teaspoon souvenirs, anything – until I had no change left, no more money at all, and was thus at the mercy of whoever was waiting for me. The air hostess insisted on giving me back ten francs so I finally bought a copper Eiffel Tower – one more souvenir of Paris. While I was making these purchases I seemed to have been delving into my handbag for about ten minutes … The bag was indeed something of a mine in which my priceless treasures were buried: a polaroid snap of Marc, book-matches from New York, a crayfish eye (for luck), and the MS of my book, which wasn't thick but weighed a ton. I was to write the last word of the latter, that one missing word, under the volcanoes. Then it would be mailed to the publisher in the Place Saint-Sulpice, Paris, which was where I used to wait for Marc (whose offices were in nearby Rue Bonaparte), pressing my nose against the window full of books with evocative titles. I can just see mine in there, *Joy* written across its navy blue cover.

The sun had scarcely risen before I was crossing the skies, flying over oceans, leaving behind whole continents. I was heading for a new galaxy. *Please fasten your seatbelts, we will be experiencing some turbulence …* And what if I never saw Paris, Meudon or the Dordogne again? Never again saw Margo, Alain, Bruce, Goraguine, my flat, or Uncle Gaspard's house? What if I died in this turbulence? What if no one was waiting for me in Wellington?

A voice uttered words I did not understand through the intercom. The tiny warning lights came on and the aircraft's nose dipped. I wanted to return to Paris. We were landing, touching down on the endless runway. I pressed my face against the circular window. Concrete flashed past, and grey hangars. I wanted to go back to Paris. I found my handkerchief and started to cry: if I'd had a father I'd never have gone. Slowly the aircraft emptied. The passengers, almost crystallised in the sudden heat, looked sympathetically at the orphan crying into her handkerchief, poor little matchgirl lost in New Zealand. I was shaking, and so distressed that the air hostess had to push me gently towards the gangway. I dried my eyes and clenched my fists (pull yourself together, Joy!) then strode out into the hot scented air.

At the foot of the gangway the deserted runway seemed to extend to infinity. No volcanoes, no palm trees. Grey concrete, blue sky, a smell of engine oil. I walked slowly towards the air terminal building, but of course I couldn't see a thing as I wasn't wearing my glasses. I would know soon enough, however.

If it were Marc I'd die of pride. If Alain, I'd die of pleasure. If Bruce, I'd die of happiness. But I'd die anyhow, wouldn't I?

I walked faster. The blurred outline drew nearer, whitish, immobile, reassuring. I could almost see him. I should see him soon.

I did see him.

Bruce.